Cameo

by

TANILLE

CAMEO. Copyright ©2006–2010 by Tanille Edwards. All rights reserved. No part of this book maybe reproduced or transmitted in any form or by any means, electrical or mechanical, including photocopying, recording or by any information storage and retrieval system, without written permission from the publisher.

For information, address Fire Flies Entertainment LLC 1077 North Avenue, Suite 114 Elizabeth NJ 07201 (212) 561-1654.

This book is a work of fiction. Names, places, characters, businesses, organizations, and incidents are either the product of the author's imagination or are used fictitiously. Any resemblance to actual persons, living or dead, locales, or events is entirely coincidental.

PRINTED IN THE UNITED STATES OF AMERICA

Cameo is a trademark of Fire Flies Entertainment LLC.
Undercover Starlet is a trademark of Fire Flies Entertainment LLC.

Published 2010

Cameo: a young adult novel/ Tanille Edwards.

Library of Congress Control Number 2010928040

ISBN 978-0-9787302-2-2

1. Young Adult – Fiction & Literature 2. Young Adult – Romance

3. Young Adult – Thriller

Table of Contents

Prelude	1
Chapter 1	16
Chapter 2	17
Chapter 3	27
Chapter 4	31
Chapter 5	42
Chapter 6	60
Chapter 7	78
Chapter 8	89
Chapter 9	106
Chapter 10	134
Chapter 11	142
Chapter 12	169
Chapter 13	176
Chapter 14	181
Chapter 15	188
Chapter 16	193
Epilogue	197

*Dedicated to a very special Latoya, Laurana, Larry,
Annie Maude, Jordan, and Justine!*

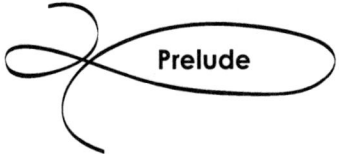

Prelude

It was pitch black outside as the full moon glistened through the vinyl blinds that adorned Gary's half window in his bedroom. His room was nestled in the far corner of his parents' craftsman-style house in Hempstead, Long Island. The scrawny seventeen-year-old sat at his desk in an oversize, droopy wifebeater and Snoopy boxer shorts. His hair was jet black and gelled down into a curly fade. His bedroom was dull, full of computer science books and a series of coveted Stephen King thrillers—a lonely boy's surrogate girlfriend.

"Uh! Got to keep these passwords straight," Gary exclaimed out of frustration.

Gary slid open his desk drawer full of colorful Post-it notes with various codes and passwords written all over them. It seemed like nowadays you needed a password for everything. There was even a code to get into his front door. He took out a new pad and wrote down a username and password for his Tracebook account. A lamp slammed to the ground behind him near his bedroom door. The bedroom went dark. Gary turned around to see what had happened. He heard footsteps in the hallway. He slapped his hand over his open mouth as if a fly might make its way inside while he trotted to the door.

Senior quarterback Craig stood outside Gary's bedroom with his back against the wall like an operative from *Mission Impossible*. Dressed in a tight, black mock-turtleneck muscle shirt, his muscles bulged like those of a beefy club bouncer.

Michelle crept up the hallway to stand next to Craig, dangling a large roll of duct tape in her hand. Craig ducked his head into the room to see what was going on. Michelle pressed her nude lips together and batted her overdone smoky eyes. She ran across the bedroom door to the opposite side. With her back to the wall, she took a look inside the room. Gary had picked up the lamp and was reaching to turn it on. *There will only be light when I say there will be light*, she thought to herself.

Michelle tugged on her black Kangol hat to signal. Craig charged into the room, grabbed a hold of Gary, and forced a pair of socks into his mouth. He pulled Gary's hands behind his back like a crooked cop from a gangster movie. Gary struggled like an insect caught in a spider web. He wiggled every which way to no avail. Michelle stood at the open bedroom door with a wicked half-smile playing across her photo-perfect, dark-chocolate face. She batted her false eyelashes for a dramatic finish.

Gary jammed his heel into Craig's toes. Craig threw Gary down onto the floor, and Michelle slammed the roll of tape against Craig's chest.

"Tape his hands up," Michelle commanded.

Craig grabbed the tape. She walked in to examine the room. "Lucy! Get in here, now!" Michelle called out.

The petite, mousy-brown-haired Lucy walked into the room looking as pale as a ghost. She had missed her last two tanning sessions to complete photo excursions for Michelle. It didn't bother her though. Lucy was just glad to have been the one asked to be in Michelle's exclusive presence. Lucy had a digital camera hanging from her wrist. The camera hung down lower than the hemline on her denim miniskirt. Lucy snapped several pictures of Gary as he squirmed on the floor. Michelle worked her way over to Gary's computer.

Craig came from behind and put his hand in Michelle's.

"This is sooo great. The yearbook committee will love it," Lucy whispered in a little girl voice. She always thought it made her seem nicer and less threatening, the complete opposite of Michelle.

"This better get me prom votes. I don't have time to waste," Michelle said.

Lucy, startled by Michelle's authoritative, slightly nasal voice, continued to take pictures of Gary rolling on the floor while he screamed curse words behind the socks stuffed into his mouth. She was aiming for just the right shot. The quandary was that she had no clue what Michelle wanted.

Lucy jumped back when Gary hurled his body toward her. "Ew-u! He keeps moving. Make him stop!" she said.

Craig kneeled on the floor and held Gary still. "Yo, are you really related to this loser?" Craig asked Michelle.

"Dude, he's just a cousin. Someone standing next to you at the tattoo spot could be your cousin. Plus he's super useful," Michelle said.

"True. Look how he's helping you get votes," Lucy surmised.

"You got a tattoo?" Craig asked.

"You haven't seen it? He hasn't seen the Bengal Tiger?" Lucy asked.

He could never find it anyway. He wouldn't even know where to look, Michelle thought to herself. She sifted through some of the files on Gary's desk.

www.UndercoverStarlet.com

"Like, I remember when I was kicked out of Girl Scouts because I told the troop leader to go to hell," Michelle said. "Then Richard …"

"You don't call him Dad? You're so crazy!" Lucy said.

"Anyway, he sentenced me to computer camp." Michelle continued.

"I didn't know you were a nerd," Craig said, offended that this was yet another thing he had no clue about. He felt like he didn't know anything about Michelle, and she didn't really care to share.

"Craig, focus," she snarled at him. Then she turned her attention to Lucy, her adoring fan. "Anyway, Gary showed me how to hook up these wicked viruses at camp."

"Stellar. Done here," Lucy said.

"Let's be out," Craig said.

"So the Gagged Nerd page is done?" Michelle asked.

"Yes. Next up, the Fashion Rejects Anonymous page," Lucy said.

"If it will get me votes." Michelle shrugged.

Lucy cut the tape off Gary's wrists. Craig cuddled up next to Michelle. "You're going to be the hottest prom queen," he said.

Maybe you could surprise me with a real adjective besides "hot," she thought to herself. But that would be like asking an old dog to learn a new trick. She yawned. As soon as she opened her mouth, Craig kissed her. She politely pushed him away. She let out a low, deep sigh.

"Duh! You guys were voted couple of the year, and you've only been dating like a month. That must be some type of

www.CameoTheNovel.com

omen that prom queen is in the bag," Lucy said.

Gary approached the three high school socialites, infuriated that he now had to comb stray cotton strands off his tongue. He grabbed Lucy by the arm. "Are you crazy?" Gary asked her.

"Handle this," Michelle instructed Craig.

"You better not publish those pictures or ... or I'm going to release some of your pre-braces pictures," Gary threatened Michelle.

"You make a threat like that, you better be able to carry it out! You don't want me to come for you, do you? I have a key to your house, Gary," Michelle said.

"That works both ways, Bitchee Michee," Gary said under his breath.

"God, you're so ungrateful," Lucy said, puzzled at Gary's apparent discontent.

Craig pushed Gary against the wall and held him there. "Calm down," Craig commanded.

"You stupid puppet. Get off me," Gary snapped. Craig slammed Gary against the wall again, then jammed his forearm under Gary's chin.

"Without us, he wouldn't even make it into the yearbook. Shame on him," Lucy said. She and Michelle exited the room. Michelle was trying her best to walk like a runway model for her audience. If her hips swung out any farther, she would be perfect for a rap video.

"Now you're going to go back to your computer geek stuff and forget this ever happened," Craig instructed.

"I don't think so!" Gary snarled.

www.UndercoverStarlet.com

Craig punched Gary in the stomach. Gary doubled over.

"I bet you think so now," Craig said as he loosened his hold hold on Gary.

Gary made his way to the violated area, otherwise known as his computer desk. Craig left quietly. As Gary grunted from the pain in his stomach, he noticed something.

"Uh! So lucky to be your cousin. Ms. Perfect, try not to lose my password next time." Gary rummaged through the pile of papers on his desk to find the password Post-it. "And get the story straight, child, because I failed programming class in computer camp. You're the one who taught me to program viruses!" Gary shouted out. But they had already left the house. He had never felt so exploited.

"I have created the group list for your term projects," yelled Mr. Sui, an overweight, bald Asian teacher dressed in an Armani suit, obviously taking himself way too seriously for public high school. "Right now, the project topic sheet is being passed around. Choose one of the four project options," he announced with a grand gesture.

"He must have been royalty in a past life, since he can't shake the act," Nia whispered to Cindy. Before the tall, sun-kissed beauty could say another word, Mr. Sui continued his oration. "Students, you can choose from the following: a five-page, double-spaced, Times New Roman—not Courier New—twelve-point font report on global economic events or an oral report including visuals suck as graphs and photos for presentation." He marched to the back of the room with his back perfectly erect and his head held high. "Or, the third choice, a skit based on an economic, historical fact that shows how changing that fact would have changed history. Or, last but not least, you may choose to do a magazine article …"

"Oh, what kind of magazine article? Can we go to, like, a *Fifteen Magazine* feature for it?" the almost-legal, triple-highlighted, big-boned, label mistress Carolina interrupted.

Mr. Sui cut his little eyes at Carolina. He was annoyed that she had cut him off without raising her hand.

"Now that I can complete my thought … You can create an article intended to be used as a reference on an economic event. In layman's terms, for the breezies and homies, the article must contain facts from a book as well as an analysis, meaning some thought on the event and its effects on the past and on the future. Seeing as how we require some real content, teeny-bopper magazines could never be a source of inspiration." He threw Carolina a smile.

Craig leaned against the lockers in the popular corridor. He was nervous. He had his hands tucked into the pockets of his letterman's jacket. Michelle clanked her $200 Jimmy Choo–inspired knock-offs all the way up to Craig. He started to breathe faster. He looked Michelle up and down wondering if he had made the right choice, though she did dress better than Nia—at least that's what the football groupies said. *That should count for something*, he thought. Craig was really feeling her skin-tight denim shorts and her form-fitted, hot-pink Undercover Starlet™ hoodie. Of course, he hadn't noticed her matching shoes, handbag, and hat. What dateable guy would? Oddly enough, that logic eluded Michelle. She expected him to remember everything she had worn for the past three weeks. She went through painstaking lengths never to wear the same thing twice in one month, not even

www.UndercoverStarlet.com

the same shoes.

"What did you page me for?" Michelle asked.

Craig shrugged his shoulders.

"This," Michelle said as she pointed to her and Craig, "is a luxury *not to be abused*."

"I wanted to holla at you. Cuz when we're together you barely even look at me. Are you mad?" Craig grabbed Michelle by the waist and pulled her to him. She jumped back.

"Are you brain dead? This is an arrangement. Get that straight! I want prom queen, and you're the key to it. If you were listening when I do speak to you, then maybe you would know this," She said. Craig's football teammate approached. Michelle quickly kissed Craig and slipped her hand in his pants' pocket.

"What up, Craig?" the teammate asked.

Craig had to momentarily disengage himself from Michelle's abrupt expression of lust to come up for air. "What up?"

The teammate stepped into his classroom. Michelle immediately pulled away from Craig and shivered slightly in disgust. "DO NOT do this again. Otherwise ... it's over!" Michelle said. She wiggled her French-manicured fingertip in Craig's face like the wand of a wicked witch.

"You think I need you?" he asked

"Right, like you have options." Michelle walked away.

He followed her. He wasn't sure what he was going to say, but he had a burning question eating at him inside. Why did she hate him? He grabbed her arm to get her to stop walking. It only angered her more. He could tell from her stare.

www.CameoTheNovel.com

Her eyes were laced with disapproval. She looked at him as if he were crowding her space.

"Why you say I don't have options? I had a girl when I got you," he said.

"What? Are you going to run back to Nia, the wholesome, popular misfit? That's a real good look. Besides, after me, she'll feel like a downgrade from first class to the cargo compartment!" Michelle walked away from Craig feeling like she had just trumped the senior king, especially since she walked away with his cell. Why use her own daytime minutes? She had to get something out of the arrangement, right?

Nia's mobile vibrated vigorously as Mr. Sui stood at his desk sorting papers with only moments to spare before his next class. Mr. Sui raised an eyebrow in Nia's direction. Embarrassed by the apparent disruption, Nia quickly took her cell out of her minuscule Undercover Starlet™ purse and hid it underneath her desk to turn it down.

"Students?" Mr. Sui said in an effort to test the class's attention, as he believed it belonged to only him. He waited until the class was completely quiet. "Pack up the sheets and go to the back of the room to get your partner's name," he continued. The class moved toward the back of the room like a herd of wild elephants that had just spotted a watering hole. All except Nia. She sat there in her seat wearing an Audrey Hepburn- style boatneck white top and sleek, dark, low-rise, slim-fit jeans coupled with Undercover Starlet™ customized logo boots to match her purse. It had never upset her that Craig never noticed her outfits. There were many guys in class whose eyes glanced her way every so often to catch a glimpse of her brushing her long dark hair over her shoulder or smiling at a funny text message.

Nia's best friend, Cindy, was a boy-crazed sexy mama

www.UndercoverStarlet.com

dressed in black leggings one size too small for her curvy, size four frame and an off-the-shoulder sweatshirt that barely covered her derriere. Her long brown hair was flat-ironed super straight. Cindy was prettier than most airbrushed magazine models, considering her flawless skin, her large eyes, and her high cheekbones. Although she enjoyed pushing and leaning against some of the school's cutest boys in the senior-only crowd at the back of the room, Cindy made her way back to Nia's seat to convince her to join in the fun.

Nia checked the text in her inbox. It read: CCCALL ME!

Peering over Nia's shoulder, Cindy asked, "Who's that?"

"No clue," Nia replied. She searched through the options in her inbox. The sender's number was private.

"It could be, like, a wrong number. This is why we should focus our attention on the cuties standing in the back of the room. Is it possible I am paired with someone as cute as me?" Cindy asked. Cindy grabbed Nia by the arm and dragged her to the back of the room.

"Oh ... my ... God! Nia and Jason? What has this world come to?" Carolina yelled. Nia and Cindy looked at each other. Carolina was their arch nemesis.

"That's what I think every time I see you," Cindy said to Carolina, all the while confident she might've been lucky with the draw as well. Jason, the six-foot-four star basketball player who looked like a young Michael Jordan with a little bit of Dwayne Wade, quickly left the room.

Cindy rushed to the back of the room with a slight bop for cool factor; she always did things she thought were cool to impress the male population that adored her body. The crowd had dispersed by the time she reached the posted list.

Steaming mad, she whispered sternly, "Who is Roger?"

In the absence of a reply she yelled, "Roger? Raise your hand now." *You should only be so lucky to be paired with me*, she thought.

"Never fails," Nia said under her breath with a smirk. She was relieved that Cindy faced as terrible a fate as her with this partner stuff.

A short boy dressed in a red and black plaid lumberjack shirt with thick bifocals that made his eyes look like black-eyed peas walked toward Cindy. To top things off he was pulling a backpack on wheels. He waved at Cindy with a warm smile on his face.

"Cindy," Roger said. He was excited to meet his new partner.

Cindy gasped. She threw her hand to her forehead and turned to Nia. "I think I might vomit. Am I flushed?" Cindy began to fan herself. The school bell rang.

"You look fine. Plus, I could never really tell if you were flushed. Your orange-peach blush overpowers any visible increase in blood circulation," Nia said with a smile. She loved to tease Cindy.

Jason stood with the popular students at the basketball lockers discussing the basketball game they had played the night before. Nia and Cindy walked past to go to their lockers located two social classes down the hallway.

Jason tapped Nia on the shoulder. "Where should I meet you to start the project?" Jason asked, looking directly into Nia's eyes. Nia stared at him, surprised his kind could even make eye contact. But, to ease her disbelief, she resolved that his interest was purely to see if she dug him. After all, every other girl in school did. Even Cindy would've dated him in

www.UndercoverStarlet.com

a heartbeat—if he asked her out, that is. Cindy only dated guys who liked her first.

"Why don't we meet at the library?" Nia said.

"Which one?" Jason asked.

"I don't know."

"Really?"

"What?"

"We can meet at my house. My little brother might get in the way a little, though. He bounces off the walls," Jason said.

"Uh ... I guess we could meet ..." Nia said.

"You a have suggestion." Jason was surprised.

"We can meet at my house," Nia said reluctantly.

"Where do you live?" Jason asked anxiously.

Nia shot him a concerned gaze. She was one of the prettiest girls in school. He was sure. "You better not be some type of stalker or anything," she said in a semi-serious, semi-cute voice, so as not to come off as a narcissist. Narcissism annoyed Nia to the core. How could someone really be consumed with just themselves when there were so many other things in the world to be concerned with that could actually benefit people, animals, or the environment? Jason opened his five-subject spiral notebook to pages completely filled with actual notes and diagrams. He quickly flipped to a blank page in the back.

"Write it down here. I can be there at 3:30 after the team meeting," he said.

Too much information, Nia thought to herself. "Okay," she said.

Jason and his basketball buddies watched Nia walk away.

"She's so stuck up, yo," said Derek, a tall, blond jock in a basketball team anorak.

"You're just hatin' cause she's not checkin' you," Jason said.

Derek's glamorous girlfriend and her junior class clique walked up to the basketball players. These girls were fiercely exotic.

"I know what you're thinkin'. It's not worth it," Derek said.

"Oh, you work for the psychic network now?" Jason said.

"Yo, wasn't she Craig's girl like a minute ago?" Derek asked.

Jason shrugged, wondering how Nia could've dated Craig. He wasn't sure if it was just him or what, but it seemed like Craig could only string together one thought per conversation. "And?"

"Word was that she thought she was all that and then, boom! He dumped her for Michelle." Derek and Craig looked at each other and cringed. Seemed like every dude knew Michelle was mean as hell—except Craig.

"Aye, you start the game on Saturday?" Vala, Derek's girlfriend's friend, asked Jason in a British accent. Jason turned slowly at the sound of her foreign-sounding voice to find a petite, curly-haired female beauty standing in his personal space.

"Yeah," he said casually.

"Then I'll be there." Vala smiled.

"Word. Where are you going to sit?" Jason asked.

"Behind you, of course! Do you want to know what I'm going to wear?"

There was that accent again, reeling him in. Vala whispered her under attire in Jason's ear.

www.UndercoverStarlet.com

"So, that's what's up?"

Vala nodded. "Might you find out what I can do in those?" Vala asked.

Derek pulled away from the public makeout session with his girlfriend. "Let's grab grub, y'all." The basketball team cheered. They moved down the hall in one large herd, like hyenas—insecure and degradingly silly, yet, underneath it all, somehow fierce on the social scene.

Vala grabbed Jason's hand, looking for a little lunch play.

"Let's skip lunch," she said as she led him down the hall toward the girl's bathroom.

Vala jumped on Jason, and kissed him in the middle of the hallway. Jason's etched muscles contracted to hold her up. He was a fine specimen of a senior indeed.

"What is this I see?" Mr. Sui yelled from the east side of the hallway. Jason immediately stopped kissing Vala. Mr. Sui moved like a king cobra down the hall in his polished, black-leather shoes. Jason dropped Vala. She quickly landed on her feet.

"Stop right there!" Mr. Sui sternly said as he approached. "This is not proper conduct for students in or out of school. This may be a time when hormones are raging, but you must conduct yourselves with discretion at the least. You should act with reservation and respect yourself!" Mr. Sui said in shock over Jason's behavior and unaware of Vala, which made the situation even worse because that meant she was an underclassman. "What happened to respect?"

"Technology," Vala replied smartly. Jason rolled his eyes at the embarrassing speech from his current teacher and Vala's antagonizing behavior. He directed his focus to the wall.

"In the Internet age, anything goes." Vala stared Mr. Sui in the eyes, unafraid of his whole parental control act.

"I will see to it that you both break this up and walk in different directions. You walk down this hall and you down this other way. Get to class." Jason and Vala looked at each other unsure of what to do or say. In the midst of their awkward moment, Mr. Sui shouted, "Now!"

Chapter 1

Damaged would describe the way I feel, literally and figuratively. By weeding out all the loser guys and waiting for the right one to really love, you think you're avoiding becoming one of those jaded girls—the girls who are cynical about love. They can't trust anyone. They think every move the opposite sex makes is just for the purpose of humiliating or hurting them for sport. Yet, somehow, I ended up becoming wreckage. I'm just what is left of a girl who used to believe in love.

Forever,
Nia

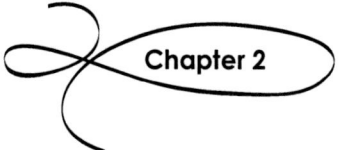

Chapter 2

The doorbell rang. I could feel my heart beating in double time. *I need to get a life!* The entertainment was here. I looked at him through the peephole. He appropriately had a swelled head through the tiny looking glass. I was hasty with opening the door. God, every bone in my body wanted to hate him.

"Hey," Jason said. I tilted my head all until I caught myself gawking at him like he was a science project. "Going to invite me in?" he asked.

"The door is open … isn't it?" I said. He stared at me blankly. "Come in," I said.

Duh! This guy definitely has some screws loose. "I've been thinking about the project," I continued. He turned and looked at me in shock. "No, really, I've been thinking about the school project," I said. He nodded his head like he understood me. Girls usually spoke in code to boys like Jason. When they said "doing" a project they usually meant "doing" him, kind of gross in a feminist kind of way. I guess he thought I was lying. Women are smart, not sex objects. We're not like guys, who think about sex every five minutes. Of course at times it seemed that no one had clued in the girls at my school about such characteristics.

"Right. I just wonder how dumb you think I am. I know I'm here for the school project. I got it, loud and clear," he said flatly.

A tiny part of me was disappointed. So there was nothing between us? I didn't want him, but I wanted him to want me, at least in light of our history. It was hard to admit there were some things I couldn't control. Being around him brought back this good feeling I used to get when I had a boyfriend. Part of me liked to stand next to a boy in all of my five-nine stature and look up at him, knowing that he dug me.

Oh, and there was the fact that at the end of sophomore year we kind of talked in between a very, very sloppy, back-of-the-staircase kiss. He never called me that summer. The next semester, I walked past him like I never knew him. Even Cindy didn't know about that. We became best friends junior year. We had a rule about secrets: If it was a secret before we met we kept it that way, but if it was a secret after we met we were obliged to dish.

He waited for me to walk through the entrance of our Art Deco dining room. I cut my eyes. That courteous crap wasn't going to fly with me. He caught a glimpse of the elaborate marble chess set in the living room. I could see he wanted to ask me something. He almost put his hand on top of mine when I reached for the chair.

"I've got it," I said. I pulled out my chair and sat down. He watched. I made sure I caught his eye when he sat down right next to me. What did he think he was doing?

"What are you doing?" I lashed out at him. Who said he could sit down right next to me? He should have sat far away, like across the table. If we were going to get this project done we needed to go over a few things. He didn't even answer me, he just sat down. But I never guessed he would bring it up.

"I lost your number. I ... I thought you were pretty and stuff ..."

Wait a minute. He thought I was pretty even when I had full

cheek acne, although I did have a mean blowdry and fly '70s flip bangs. I couldn't believe I was becoming one of those superficial girls I disdained just to prove I was too fly for him. By the way, I haven't used the word *fly* this much since sixth grade. This was going nowhere but down.

"Save it. It's just fine. We're seniors. That was a long time ago," I said.

I could see in his eyes he didn't believe me. "The economy is in a recession, an undiagnosed recession. That's a hot topic," I said.

"Nia, I'm not trying to get you back," he said.

My mouth dropped. It was like a slap in the face. "We weren't even dating!" I yelled.

"I just want you to know what happened. I would never not call a girl. Especially one like you… Look, I lost your number in my locker or something the day of my last final. I just couldn't find it. I called everyone I knew, but apparently you weren't social—at least that's what one of my boys said."

Jason wanted to say who said it. I could see it in his face. Was he blaming me for him not calling me? Can we say

"So it would have been better for several other boys at school to have my number? Hmm. What kind of girls do you deal with?"

Jason shook his head. "Nah, it's not like that. That was rude. I'm sorry."

"So what ideas do you have for the project? Me being a social recluse and all, I don't get out much. But I do fill up on CNBC. What's your source? *Sports Illustrated*?" I said.

"I didn't think of any on the way here," he said,

disappointed that his lack of a topic suggestion proved me right, that he was behind the ball.

My eyes searched his face. I had promised myself I wouldn't be a jaded cliché. You know, girl's boyfriend breaks up with her and girl hates all boys. He was looking at me but not the way I wanted him to. "I was wrong," I said.

"That was big of you."

Now I was the one who was shocked. That was something I would totally say. I laughed lightly under my breath.

"Um ... I'll do some research on the current economic conditions ... Gas prices, retail sales, stock market points," Jason said.

"I'll check into real estate prices, analyst opinions, and federal reserve interest rate news," I said.

He was taking detailed notes. He looked at me then down at my hands, as if he expected me to do the same.

"Let's say we'll collect one year's worth of research," I added.

"All right." He sighed as if he was relieved. "I'll do some tonight."

"Me, too," I said. I pushed my chair back, and he flew out of his seat. He pulled my seat out a little more.

"I got it," he said.

"It's already out."

He held his hand out.

"I can get out of my seat by myself. This isn't 1890."

Yet again he looked at me, disappointed.

"But thank you."

How could this guy make me feel so ... so unnecessarily

sarcastic? The problem with knowing you're being sarcastic is feeling like you're missing out on his reaction if you'd been nice. It's a good thing I didn't have to admit these feelings to anyone out loud. He trailed just three steps behind me all the way to the front door.

"So I'll see you tomorrow. I didn't mean it the way it sounded. I'm not inviting myself. Um, but I will be here tomorrow, if that's the plan," he said.

So I wasn't the only one feeling like she was under a microscope. I turned to him, and he kept moving toward me. Before I knew it, he was all up in my area.

I confess. It took all the strength I had to reach for the door at that moment. He put his hands out in between us like he didn't want us to touch or to run into each other. "Uh, sorry. You just stopped."

"Am I to blame for everything?" I asked.

He just shook his head and smiled. "Later."

He touched my shoulder like I was a football buddy, then my blood started to boil. Wait, that's basketball buddy. It's all coming back to me. I remembered why exactly I hated his type and why I should not get excited at the sentiment of his touch even if it was masked as a chummy goodbye. I slowly slid his hand off my shoulder. I didn't want to accuse him of wanting me again. At this point who cared?

"Goodbye." I closed the door behind him. Too bad that wasn't the last of him.

Less than a minute later, my mother strolled in like the happy camper she usually was. My mother was one of those moms that your boyfriend hoped you'd look like twenty years later, if you were still together. She was elegant, fashionable, and sophisticated. She was like a young Diahann

Carroll.

"So I see someone has a new boyfriend," she said.

Did I mention she was a lawyer and that, at times, she tactlessly got right down to the nitty-gritty? "What were you doing home alone?" Note to self: Next time Jason comes over for homework make sure to dress like it's a homework date, i.e., sweats and a ponytail. Did I just say date? Great! As long as I didn't say it out loud.

I signed in on Tracebook online. I had a friend from my internship last summer—well, it was more like a volunteer-type, candy-striping gig, but around college application time, we seniors have to get a little creative with our extracurricular activities. She was more like me than anyone at school. I had to check to see if she was online. She would get this whole Jason thing. I took a momentary pause to acknowledge the fact that merely getting on Tracebook to talk was admitting that there was a "thing" going on with Jason. It was like a bad chemical reaction, however those were usually followed by some sort of rash or patchy skin thing—yuck. If I could associate kissing him with that rash then all would be well.

My mom snuck up behind me. "Nee, you wouldn't believe it. The screen on my laptop went out today. Kelly, my new assistant was setting up for a client meeting, when, boom, it was out. Luckily, we had borrowed the newbie's laptop for the presentation. His was brand-new. So where's your BFF? That is what you're calling your best friends these days, true … or false?" she said.

"Only if we're on a first-name basis, Susan."

"Oh, honey, don't call me that. There is only one person in the world that gets to call me Mom. It's special."

That's also what she told me about my virginity. The "It's

special" line was multipurpose. I now see.

My mom searched through her mail like there was a letter bomb in there. She carefully examined each piece by throwing it around with a pen before she even picked it up. That's what too many forensic crime shows amount to these days: being petrified of your own mail. We all have our compulsions. I wash my hands with that antibacterial stuff in a tube after I touch money, doorknobs, and anything on the public transit system.

Gary66? Who the heck was that?

"hey, remember me from last year? we sat in the back of English together. i searched your name, and this profile popped up so i thought it must be Amber," Gary66 said on instant message.

First off, I don't even know anyone who sends instant messages with all lowercase except for the words English and Amber.

"He's cute. What's his name?" my mom asked.

"Who?"

"The guy who just left the house." She knew I knew who she meant.

"Jason." I wasn't looking at her, but from the lack of response, I would say her mouth had just dropped.

"Hmmm. I guess you finally got some answers out of him," she said.

"How petty. Though he did explain himself. And, yeah, some girls think he's cute. But he's ..." It was hard to sum him up in just one word. My voice trailed off as I turned my attention to Gary66's next message.

"what the deal? u there. says you're online."

"Hello, Gary66. No, I am not Amber and no I do not know an Amber. Do not instant message me," I replied.

Man, this was turning out to be some kind of day. Some days I could actually be sweet, or so I've been told.

"sorry, who ruined your day? sounds like a guy did it. i know cause that's usually how the story goes. boy breaks girl's heart and, well, girl gets bitter."

"I am blocking you now. Guess I wear bitter well," I answered back.

Who did Gary66 think he was? All of a sudden, I was supposed to confess? IHD (in his dreams)—if we're talking in alleged text messaging talk. I've watched one too many cell phone commercials. Now I think I can make up my own text acronyms.

Just as I turned away from the computer screen I saw her do it. She moved her knight to kill my castle. Then my mom smugly left the living room. I bet she thought she was a genius when she was growing up. My mom was way too humble to admit it, but every once in a while I caught a glimpse of her smug nature and just wondered...did I crush all that? I moved my queen to take her knight.

"Check," I said. My mom ducked her head into the living room. She looked at me out of the corner of her eye like I was a guilty defendant under questioning.

"M.O.M., what's for D.I.N.N.E.R.?" I asked to purposely mock her.

"T.O.," she said.

"I'll dial," I said. It was going to be our Tuesday special. Shrimp with broccoli and brown rice. "Ordering from my room."

"By the way, Craig called yesterday while you were at the bookstore."

"And what do you think he wants? To apologize? Reconcile? No. No. Maybe his IQ has gone up a point or two over the past month. Stranger things have happened."

"Be civil, honey."

I furrowed my eyebrows as if to say I would have none of that.

"One last thing, Nee. I'm flying out to Atlanta the day after tomorrow. I'm leaving right after work for a meeting on Thursday. I'll be back Friday. I want you to stay at your grandparents' house."

"You mean with Nana and Papa?" Nana was my father's mother. Though my father lived halfway across the country, spending the summers with his overprotective, controlling personality wasn't enough. Any chance my mother got she pushed me to see my Nana. You might picture an older, *Wheel of Fortune*-, *Price Is Right*-watching, I-shop-with-a-zillion-coupons-in-my-fanny-pack Nana. Wrong. Nana was a tell-you-what-to-do, she-knows-best type of couture diva who took more cruises than a college student at a B-list school during all of his summer breaks combined. She was too high maintenance for me.

"Can't Cindy come over? Can we stay here one night and then stay at her house one night or whatever? Plus Nana said ... she's going away soon. You know how she likes to shop before she goes on a big trip."

Was there any other outlandish reason I could come up with that played up Nana's unusual social schedule for a seventy-something?

www.UndercoverStarlet.com

"No, Nia. You are not going to stay home by yourself. Two teenagers don't equal one adult."

"But she's my BFF."

This time I wasn't the one cutting my eyes. You'd think my mother was the one who had originated the eye stare popularly known as a dirty look.

"Let Cindy meet you here and you both go over to her house," she said.

"Okay."

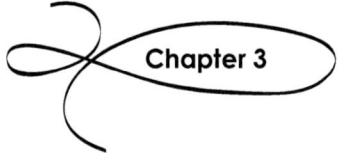

Chapter 3

I had just gotten this new CD. I was addicted to this new era of R&B. Anyway, my meticulous room was filled with '80s vinyl, '90s CDs, a huge stereo system, and my MP3 player. I was in the process of downloading all my CDs onto my MP3 player. I tried not to look at my picture wall when I was searching for my dazzling, superstar nightgown. Nana had brought it for me last Christmas. She had left the price tag on. I didn't know if she forgot it or if she was just ostentatious. That was a tough one.

My room was super cool. I painted it gold just last month. It was like my rebirth after I broke up with Craig. It was great because when I woke up every morning the sun reflected off the metallic-gold walls. It reminded me of art. Sometimes I'd just lie on the hardwood floors warmed by the sun, staring up at the ceiling with my feet up against the wall like a yogi. In those moments life seemed great. It felt full of possibilities and, to be honest, I felt free. Not having a boyfriend was a double-edged sword. Sometimes you felt good about being free. It was just you and the world. Then at other times, you felt like only half of yourself because you couldn't express the part of you that wanted to shower someone else with love. How easily my mind segued from one philosophical moment to the reality of the present.

There was a gaping hole on my wall of pictures. A hole I hadn't closed just yet. Like the hole in my heart. As smoothly as things had gone earlier, it was apparent that I wasn't ready to fill my heart either. But right there, between the picture of me and Cindy dressed like chic pirates for Halloween and the picture of me and the inside of a locker decorated with rainbows and My Little Ponies was a space. That was sophomore year. Every so often, I liked to be reminded that I was once sweet enough to like My Little Pony. I thought I spotted Craig's hand in a picture of me and a group of girls in the lunchroom so I took the picture down. Those girls weren't girls at all. They were wenches who dumped me right along with Craig. That space in the wall was my inspiration. Never again would I fool myself into thinking anything in high school could be real.

My mom knocked on my door. Before I could say "open," there was her head peeking in.

"Goodnight, Nee," she said.

"Goodnight, Mom." I hugged my mom for all the trying she did. She was really down, but I would never tell her that. She closed the door. She left me to my CDs and my mirror. So, okay, I admit sometimes I liked to pretend I was in my own music video. Ah, but I just needed a cup of water. I never go to bed without a cup of water. Just as I was walking to the door, my mother knocked again. She popped in with a gleaming glass of fresh spring water in hand. She left the door open.

"My cameo lover, my cameo lover. You came to make a cameo in my life. Used to love the way you smile then go bye-bye," I sang into the mirror.

I only really knew the first two sentences of the song but, hey, I was on beat and sounding kind of good. Rewind. "My cameo lover, my cameo ..." I went to my door and looked down the long hallway both ways. If my eyes weren't playing tricks on me, someone had just run past my room and giggled. Ew-u, who giggles "he, he, he"? It was so weird. Was that supposed to be sinister? I couldn't believe I was attempting to rationalize this. It would be preposterous even if it were true. Sufficed it to say that was the last I playing the CD that night.

Maybe my mom had run down the hall. I ran through our narrow hallway to my mother's room. I knocked on her door, desperate for an answer. "Did you run down the hall?"

"What?"

"I thought for a second, this is going to sound crazy, but I just saw someone run past my room and giggle."

She rubbed her eyebrows. That was the signal that she was too tired for this nonsense. "I will check the house, but I am sure no one ran past your room and giggled."

She mocked me with air quotations around the word "giggled." She went down the hall to check the closets and the guest bedroom. She turned on all the lights. She went downstairs.

I knew what she was really thinking. Why couldn't I be like other teenage girls, in my room text messaging my boyfriend until sunrise and leaving my parents to sleep? No, I had to be the karaoke-singing type of girl who caught every detail of every little thing.

"You know we have an alarm. I put it on when I went to get your glass of water," she said as she walked up the stairs. I pulled back the heavy sea-blue curtains on her windows. Her room had an ocean-inspired theme. Everything in it was the color of the ocean or the plants and coral reef.

"Just sleep here tonight," she said.

I looked out the other window on the other side of her room. All I could see was the neighbor's back yard. I wondered just what this giggling fool looked like. I remembered overalls and a black turtleneck. I think the face was black too. Like a ski

www.UndercoverStarlet.com

mask? Doubt had the best of me. I was too scared to think about what it would mean if I was right. Yet being wrong could mean I needed psychiatric help. Who would dream up some sort of giggling, farmer creep running past her door?

Huh, yet another thing that separated me from the general population.

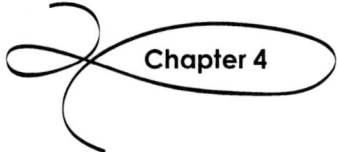

Chapter 4

"Do you have a pen?" Cindy asked Peter as she flipped her hair to one side and brushed back the stray hairs with her fingers.

"Uh … oh." He could barely form a word. He scrambled through his junky backpack and pulled out a fancy pen. It looked practically new. I guess he'd been saving it for something special.

"Right here." Cindy pointed to a spot right above her collar bone. She pulled her camisole strap off her shoulder to show more skin. Cindy tilted her neck as Peter snuggled up against her to write his phone number above her collar bone. He smiled the whole time.

"You smell good," Peter said.

Please! As if that wasn't the most trite flirting line ever uttered by a boy.

"Like what?" Cindy asked as she pulled her shirt strap back onto her shoulder. She was playing him like a violin. She knew exactly what strings to pluck. And like the many before him, he was melting in the palm of her hand. She had tried to teach me how to play guys like that. It wasn't quite my style. That and I wasn't such a quick study when it came to flirting. But the makeup details I had down pat. We always wore a little bit of base, black mascara, and black eyeliner inside the eye only. Guys couldn't tell the difference—they just thought you had great skin and dark eyes. To me, the look was just as important as the flirt. Plus, I didn't like to work for a date. I preferred my date to work for me. In other words, I always played hard to get.

I couldn't help but turn my attention to the two freshman girls wearing step team uniforms—the T-shirts that said STEP TEAM were a dead giveaway. What were these girls whispering about? Probably Cindy and Peter. For freshman girls, senior boys were like the dating jackpot. I began to fidget with the books in my locker. I really had no reason to keep it open, but I wanted to know more about what was on their minds.

"Where is it?" I said to myself. I rummaged through my locker, looking for the mysterious thing that was supposedly missing. Then I heard it! Just when I thought all the whispers had been quelled.

"Michelle. Yeah! She stole her boyfriend," one girl said. I couldn't make out every detail, but whatever they were whispering was definitely about me. What in the heck gave them the right to go around spreading rumors?

I slammed my locker shut. The freshman neophytes just stood there staring at me.

"That happened like a month ago!" I said. I was so tired of defending myself. "Close your mouths. That's not very ladylike."

Surprisingly, they did as I said. "You know, that jacket is fire on you," I whispered coyly. From the looks on their faces, I had just gone from a name to an experience. Talk about that! Sometimes I even surprised myself. There are times when the only way to combat negative energy is with a compliment.

Next thing I knew, Cindy was nestled in the corner with Peter hovering over her. "Call me with the details," I texted her. "Absolutely," she texted back. I guess it was me and the bus today.

Outside, I walked up the block alone. Usually there were masses of kids walking home or to the burger spot on the corner. Most of the kids were well on their way by now. Whatever about the anonymous school kids, I was still trying to shake off what had happened the night before.

"So, we meeting up today?" an unmistakable voice said.

There he was looking like he was straight out of a varsity calendar in a short-sleeved shirt, showing just enough of his muscles to make you look. He pulled his cherry-red Mustang convertible over and jumped out. I was a little nervous, not to mention slightly annoyed. I was hoping to have some time to myself to sort things out. I wasn't sure what to do—stop and talk or keep walking. I chose the latter.

"What makes you think that I don't have plans? I'm not your garden-variety type of nerd. I'm a hybrid. Evolved," I said.

"Sophisticated. I get it."

"I could be doing something this evening that I have to get prepared for," I said.

He jumped back into his car and drove beside me, following me. "All right, I wasn't trying to be weird. I didn't know," he said.

"Oh, no, I'm not busy. It's just a possibility. The kind of thing you would never know if you didn't ask ... Why do you look so confused?" I asked.

"I am. You said something about preparing," he said.

"Forget that, you can meet me at my house," I said.

"Well, get in. I'll drive."

"No. Thanks. My bus pass works just fine."

www.UndercoverStarlet.com

"Stop playing."

"I'm not playing."

"I'm staying here until you get in."

"Well that won't be long. Here's the bus. Maybe you should get out of the bus stop," I said.

He shrugged and pulled out.

The bus doors closed behind me. I showed my pass and that was it. I was free to sit anywhere. I picked a seat by the window on the side where the sun was shining. Me and the sun, it was special. Sometimes I felt like sitting in the sunlight melted all the crazy stuff away. Little did I know that the one seat available on that side of the bus had a blinding view of the sun. After retreating to the comfort of my big, dark sunglasses, my eyes landed on Jason. He was driving alongside the bus. Although I tried to read my English Lit book, the sharper faculties of my brain seemed more focused on whether or not anyone could see my eyes through my shades than Thoreau. I couldn't help but sneak a peak at him at every red light and sometimes in between. I caught him looking up at the bus every once in a while. I quickly turned my head, so that my neck craned in his direction wouldn't give me away.

I wondered if he knew which bus stop I got off at. My stop was next. When I looked out the window, he was gone. I wish I could say I was relieved, but I try not to be too self-delusional. I mean, we all lie to ourselves at one point or another—sometimes for our own good, or to protect our ego, or to ease the hurt of a bad memory. But to do it on a daily basis could be dangerous, I think. Sometimes I feel like a thirty-year-old psychologist living in a teenager's body.

I was off the bus and heading up my block. The bus had long passed me by and was well on its way to the next stop.

The exhaust of the bus had cleared. I looked over my shoulder casually. I guess I was expecting that he would be there, riding alongside me, but he wasn't. Oh, well. The closer I got to my house, the more vivid the image of the red coupe parked in front of my neighbor's house became. Suddenly I found myself walking at light speed. Great! The last thing I needed to do was speed walk from the bus stop. He would only think I was rushing to my door to see him.

There was really no way of walking to my door without passing him.

"Hey," he said as he jumped out of the car.

"Hello," I said. I noticed my mother's car was in the driveway. Great.

"Do you want to study?" he asked.

Hadn't I already invited him over? "You're here, right? Might as well make the best of it," I said. I could feel my heart skip a beat when I let him through the door.

This was all wrong, but it was sort of hard to be mad at him all the time.

I brought my laptop into the living room so we could do some research.

"Nia," my mother said. I wondered if whether I ignored her she would just leave me alone. "Nia." She hurried into the living room. Behind her my little cousin, Lacey, followed. "There you are, honey. Studying today?"

"Yes, Mom. Jason this is my mother and my little cousin, Lacey," I said.

Jason shook my mother's hand. "How are you, ma'am?" he asked.

www.UndercoverStarlet.com

"I'm fine. Call me Ms. Stevens," she said.

"How are you, Lacey?" Jason shook her hand too. He was weird.

"Just fine, thank you."

Oh, gosh, had I just seen my little cousin bat an eye?

"Why don't you get Jason some of your peach cobbler?" my mother insisted.

"Jason, um, I can get you a piece," I said.

"Nah, we can finish this. Maybe later we can get some," he said.

An instant messenger screen popped up on my computer. Gary66 wanted to add me to his buddy list. I thought I blocked him the other day. I closed out the window quickly. Then my computer just shut off. Jason and I looked at each other. Somehow my mother and Lacey had found their way out of my space. It was a miracle.

"You could just turn it back on," Jason said.

"It was plugged in. Why would it just die?" I said.

"Calm down. There is nothing wrong with it," Jason said.

"I didn't say there was. But we need the Internet to work." I turned the computer back on. Some strange screen I'd never seen before came up. Something on my C drive was corrupted. I had to run a repair program before it would complete the boot-up.

"I have that virus software on my computer too. It's a good program," he said.

"Thanks." It took every shred of restraint I had for me not to break out into a full panic. I had everything on my laptop. For a minute or two, I couldn't move. I couldn't believe it had just shut down like that. Just when I thought my vision of the snickering farmer was my worst nightmare.

"This could be okay, right? I mean this program running is a good sign?" I said.

"Be cool," Jason said.

"I run a virus scan every week! What happened?"

"Maybe it has something to do with that instant message," Jason said.

"I don't even know that person. I have two firewalls on this computer!" I said.

"Just let the computer do its thing. I have this program. It'll be fine. Trust me."

I dropped my head in my hands. I needed to think. This was crazy. Five minutes ago everything was fine. I was just so nervous. I had even started typing some of the work for our report. I had it saved on my computer. It felt like all of a sudden my laptop had me by the jugular.

"What about some peach pie?" Jason asked.

"What? At a time like this?" I asked.

Jason sighed.

"It's cobbler, anyway," I said.

"Yes, that's it, cobbler," Jason said.

I couldn't stop starring at my computer.

"The hourglass means it's still working. We'll come back," Jason said. He led me away from the computer, through the dining room into the kitchen. My eyes were glued to the floor as I pondered, Why me?

My mother had left the cobbler on the counter. I guess she

figured we'd make our way into the kitchen at some point. I cut us two pieces in silence.

"You cook often?" Jason asked.

"I don't know. Maybe. Here and there."

Jason took his first bite of the cobbler. "You made this from scratch?"

"Yeah."

"You could be a chef," he said.

I laughed.

"Not a chef, then. What are you going to study in college?" he asked.

"I don't know yet. I'm undecided"

"Word? I thought you had it all figured out."

"What about you?"

"I'm studying law."

"Really? You? A lawyer?"

"Well, I'm going to be a political science major anyway, and I'll see. Four years is a long time."

"That's true. I don't know. I always imagined that I would be a writer someday. I want to write a detective series about an undercover sleuth. I love mysteries," I said.

"You could study literature," Jason said.

"I know, but I like so many things. I really like science. I might want to be a biochemist. And I could write in my spare time," I said.

"I still think you should be a chef. This pie is off the chain," Jason said.

"So I told you something about me, what about you? What do you like to do?"

"I cook a little. ... Nah, I can't even boil water. I kayak. Have you ever been kayaking?"

"Kayaking? No."

"In the summer, I go with my father and my little brother."

"You have a little brother?"

"Yup. He's six. He loves boats. If you bring some pie with you, I could maybe show you how to kayak one day," Jason said.

"Maybe one day I might go. Is the pie my admission fee?" I asked.

"Yup. Something like that." Guys were always making promises they didn't intend to keep. "I'm going to …"

"Okay," I abruptly cut him off. I needed to end that conversation about our future. What future? I walked to the living room. He followed. I snapped up his backpack. He got on my computer and opened the file we had just been working on. I thought he was leaving.

"Here's the stuff we worked on. See? It's all good," he said.

"What are you doing?" I asked.

"Emailing it to myself," he said. "I'll work on it at home tonight."

"Well … I'll do some work tonight too."

"Okay. I'll hit you up on email then," he said.

"Definitely hit me up," I said. I followed him to the door.

"Um … all right then," he said as he grasped the strings on his mountain backpack. Guys thought that was fashionable. An $80 backpack meant for hiking in the mountains can carry two books at most.

"Okay," I said.

"Good evening," he said.

"So formal." I laughed.

He cleared his throat. Could it be? Did I make him nervous? I stepped out onto the porch. We stood there face to face.

"Good evening," I mocked him.

He looked away from me, embarrassed.

"What's with the extra storage?" I tugged at his backpack.

"You never know when you're going to snap someone up in your passenger seat and need to carry an extra book or two in your backpack," he said.

I pretended the meaning of that had totally eluded me. I found myself wanting to kiss him on the cheek. Damn it! I hated that I was so susceptible to a cute smile and compliments on my cobbler. He seemed so available. Yet I knew better. Guys like him always had girlfriends. Not that I cared so much, it wasn't my place—I wasn't in the market for a date.

Too soon had I forgotten how he had kissed me and never called. He slowly walked down the porch steps backwards. I just watched him. The more I said, the more he would think I liked him. I had to nip this in the bud. He made it down the steps and all the way to the curb, successfully keeping one eye on me the whole time. I had to give it to him, he was definitely smooth. He waved at me before I watched him walk to his car and pull off. His smile was kind. It almost made him seem trustworthy. Part of me thought he would be the kind of boyfriend who would stop at nothing to please me. But I wouldn't let him get me all loopy. I couldn't let him change me. How could that thought even cross my mind? Kayaking?

What reasonable teenager went kayaking?

I had promised myself not to think of him the rest of the night. Just when I thought the last four weeks of school were going to be a breeze, the plot was beginning to thicken.

By now, I had hoped to chalk up that farmer giggle thing to my imagination. There were more pressing things on my mind. Right? Wrong! Buried in my deepest fears was that it wasn't something that I had imagined. But I kept those fears socked away in my subconscious right along with the fear that I would end up a jobless loser after high school unable to complete college for no apparent reason. Upon recalling such a scary thought I decided to get myself a bowl of ice cream and go to bed early.

Chapter 5

Thank goodness for the bell. Our electronic school bells were, like, the best inventions since sliced bread. They were always on time. First period was about to start in five minutes. Cindy and I walked down the nosebleed section of lockers where all the misfits, ex-jocks, wannabe cheerleaders, punk rockers, and the socially anxious hid from the rest of the school. Personally, I think lockers should be assigned rather than chosen so we could all learn to get along and appreciate each others' differences. But the idea of an over-talkative, Red Bull–addicted, burnt-out cheerleader accosting me every time I needed to go to my locker did sort of weird me out.

"I so need to clean out my locker," Cindy said. She dumped her books at the top of the locker. She had two pairs of shoes, three pairs of jeans, a minimal number of books, and a cosmetics bag the size of a small suitcase stuffed into her locker.

"Okay, don't think I'm weird," I said.

"Too late for that."

"Well …" I paused to think about the psychological ramifications of revealing that I might have imagined the whole thing. "I think I saw someone run past my bedroom and snicker the other night."

Let's just say Cindy couldn't contain herself. You would've thought she'd invented uproarious laughter there in that moment.

That wasn't the reaction I was hoping for.

"Okay. Change the subject. How's Roger working out?"

Though I knew Cindy wanted to know more about the phantom snicker, I also knew she could never pass up an opportunity to rant about how she had yet again been wronged by Mr. Sui. Cindy's face quickly turned from a smile to a serious grimace. Such a choice left me wanting more than ever to hash this thing out. I woke up this morning with the snicker on my mind. I needed to talk about this with someone.

"I just want you to know I have made major sacrifices for the benefit of my college career! I had to give that wheelie-carrying nerd my phone number. He text messages me once every hour."

"Uh, maybe he's working really hard on the project."

"Cut the crap. Save it for your presentation," Cindy said.

I did feel a little sorry for him. The glamourati of our school were far more screwed up than he was. "He's not that bad. He has a genuine smile. You can't fake a genuine smile," I said.

"If I was thirty and desperate maybe that line would work. As of now, I'm unconvinced," Cindy said.

"Thirty is my scary age too!" I said.

"We met in study hall this morning, before second period, and he sat so close to me I could feel his breath on my cheek. By the way, it reeked of broccoli! Who eats broccoli for breakfast?" Cindy said.

"He does have braces," I said.

Cindy let out a long sigh. "That is so gross," she said.

"Think happy thoughts! Think of Peter," I said.

I caught Michelle eyeing us. She walked by with her two

sidekicks. "Did you see the new charm bracelet Craig gave me? One for each day we kissed before we were official," Michelle yelled across the hallway.

Michelle was this girl I had never even noticed before Craig. Even when we dated I never talked to her. I might've seen her around once or twice. It's like she fell out of the sky onto the scene.

"Oh. Wow. This is so great," Lucy said in her whiny voice. It was like listening to nails scratch a chalkboard. Michelle pushed Lucy into me.

"Excuse you," I said.

"Does anybody hear the sound of ex-football trash?" Lucy asked Michelle and Michellette, an unidentifiable Michelle mini-me whose sole purpose in life was to laugh at Michelle's jokes. To think that in the rank of airheads there could be someone lower on the scale than Lucy.

"They should only be so blessed we've even passed by the loser row of lockers," Michelle said. "Witch," she whispered when she walked pass me. I had had enough. I definitely wasn't the witch in this situation.

I stopped Michelle right in her tracks. Face to face she wasn't all that. Not even close. I hated her full set of fake lashes, full face powder foundation, and overdone eye shadow and blush. No one who was really pretty needed all that makeup. "I didn't catch that."

"Oh, do you mean the witch part? Funny that you didn't get it. It was aimed at you," Michelle said as she dangled her finger in my face. In my mind, I had grabbed her arm and guided her hand to cover her mouth. She needed to shut her trap! But instead I just rolled my eyes.

www.CameoTheNovel.com

"Why don't you just shut up!" I said. Surprisingly she did.

"That's much better," Cindy said.

"You may think twice about name calling. You see, while you've been brainstorming on names to call me your boyfriend has been calling me every night for the past ... I'd say, week!" I yelled.

Every rumor-disseminating girl stopped in her tracks and pulled out her cell phone immediately. "Oh! She blew up your man's spot!" Cindy said.

"You may have a couple of uncomfortable stares coming your way. Enjoy lunch," I said to Michelle. I brushed past that witch. She laughed strangely under her breath. She was sort of creepy in a way you just couldn't put your finger on. Craig walked up behind Michelle and put his hand around her waist. "Hey, baby girl," he said. His voice was so deep it gave me chills. And then there was that hint of scratchiness in it. I had to catch myself. Craig was all about the show. The type of guy who walked down the hall with his laptop open playing music and bopping his head in the crowded hallway rather than using his MP3 player to play music discreetly.

"Hi, baby boy," Michelle said slowly as if she hoped I could hear. I wouldn't have even been privy to their cuddling escapade if I hadn't had to look for Cindy. I thought she was right behind me.

"You need to control your chick," Cindy said to Craig. Then she whispered in his ear, "And stop calling Nia. It's a really bad look."

"Cindy, come on," I said.

The longer I had to look at him, the more disgusted I became. What made him think he had a right to constantly request my attention by constantly calling me? I hoped he was painfully sorry. I hoped that his heart felt like something had rotted to the core. He was so wack! What irked me more than him calling me was that he sure didn't look sorry.

Michelle growled at Cindy

"Take her to the ASPCA. She needs to be put down for the betterment of mankind," Cindy said to Craig.

"Was Craig wearing a black turtleneck?" I asked.

Cindy looked worried. "Yeah. He's worn that, like, I don't know how many times," she said.

"I try to block all memories of him. I never directly look at him for fear I might turn to stone. Have you ever seen him in overalls?" I asked.

"Overalls? No. Why?" she asked.

Just when I was about to cautiously answer, there was that trusty bell again.

"Nia!" Jason called out.

I turned around and he was sprinting toward me.

"You're so good with the athletes. Tell him to hook me up with one of his friends ... if you come up for air," Cindy said.

"Please, I'm heading to lunch," I said.

"You know that's your boo," Cindy said as she glanced at her watch. "I can't be late for Spanish. My parents are all over me about learning to speak Spanish. It's good for a job, they say. Whatever. If I didn't sit next to that gorgeous guy from the school paper, forget about it. That class would be about as exciting as ..." Cindy said. She was at a loss for words.

"... As watching paint dry. I know. I took that class last semester," I said.

"Hey. What up?" Jason said.

"Nothing is going to stand between me and the hot editor boy. Holla ..." Cindy's voice trailed down the hall. She left me to deal with the track star. I walked away from him. He followed.

"Did you get the work I emailed you last night?" he asked.

I pulled his email up on my cell phone. Then I showed it to him.

Carolina rammed her big hips in the crawl space between us. I turned right back around and marched to the girl's bathroom at the end of the hall. Carolina was kind of warped. She and Jason might make a good couple. She was the type of girl who considered the words "I want to marry you one day" uttered by a guy in a heated moment as a bona fide proposal. A teenage boy changes his mind as often as he changes his kicks. Talk about weird. What kind of girl, in the age of touch-pad mobile phones, Internet television, and supersize this or kiddie size that, still believed she would get married at 19 and stay married forever? She thought that by hanging around a guy long enough he'd just give in and confess his secret passion for her. I wished someone would bring her into the 21st century and tell her she resembles more of a groupie than anything. Of course, had she not spilled her guts to the entire locker room during gym two semesters ago I wouldn't know this stuff.

I walked into the bathroom. I looked back down the hall in his direction, and his eye caught mine. I abruptly turned my head only to get knocked in the nose by a freshman on the opposite side of the door pushing the door outward.

"Ouch!" I said.

"Oh, I am so, so sorry," the freshman stuttered.

I looked in the mirror. Not a bruise in sight. "It's okay." I smiled.

"Are you …"

Was this freshman going to ask me the age-old question every senior worth a grain of salt in the popularity stratosphere had seen fit to ask me just a mere four weeks ago? I eyed her like a hit man eyes his mark.

"… Going to use that stall? Cause ain't no toilet paper in there," she continued.

"Thanks." I turned my back and let out a sigh under my breath. I thought she was going to ask me if I was the girl Craig had dumped.

"Is everything all right?" she asked. The sound of her voice was beginning to make me flinch—and what was with the dramatic echo in that bathroom?

When I looked her way, she was gone. The bathroom door swung back and forth. My mother had put all that forensic stuff in my head, so the inner skeptic in me had to check underneath each bathroom stall to make sure no one else was there. The moment I stood up there was a howling sound coming from the window. Had that been open before? Just as I closed it and intended to get right down to the business of using the bathroom and getting out of there, out of the corner of my eye I spotted something on the mirror. It wasn't my reflection that did it. It was the red letters that spelled CAMEO. That was it for me. Proof! Finally!

I ran to the door swiftly and gave it a good push. It was stuck. It felt like there was a 500 pound hill on the other side. I kept pushing as hard as I could until I realized I was sliding. I had to perch on the corner of the boyfriend graffiti wall, an old roster of who used to date whom, to prevent myself from falling into the pool of red ... punch? Had that punch mysteriously accumulated at the bottom of the doorway in the past three minutes while I'd been in the bathroom?

Someone was trying to punk me. Why? I gained my balance by leaning my back against the wall by the door. I kicked the door as hard as I could. It swung open so fast I had to quickly leap out of the bathroom for fear it might swing back the other way and knock me down. I guess that 500 pound rock standing at the door was now gone. Suffice it to say I tracked red stickyfoot prints all the way to my next class.

By the end of the day, I had a sense of terror inside of me. I rinsed off my tennis shoes and settled for squeaking up and down the hallway rather than sticking to it. Jason was waiting for me at my locker. This boy was like concierge services. Did he intend to drive me home?

"So," he said. He bobbed his head up and down while he thought of something to say.

"So," I said. Naturally, I bobbed my head like him and thought of what to say next. "Did you have anything to do with the prank that went on in the bathroom earlier?" I asked.

"No. What prank?" he asked.

"How would you know that I was going to go to the bathroom at that time, is what I'm trying to figure out," I continued.

He laughed. "I don't know what the deal is with the bathroom, and who said I care what you do?" he said.

I shoved my books into my locker and quietly closed it. I didn't want my slamming it to be mistaken as anger. "I'm ..." I couldn't believe I was saying this. "Sorry," I said.

He laughed. "Was that hard for you?" he asked.

"That and having someone lock me in the bathroom and

pour punch underneath my feet. Not to mention thinking I saw someone in my bedroom the other night." I paused for a breath knowing that I had said too much. Note to self: Learn how to keep a secret. I could see the wheels in his head turning. "Did you tell this to the dean?"

"By the time I would've gone to show them, it probably would've been cleaned up!"

"Tomorrow I'm walking you to all of your classes until we find out who this is," he said. For a moment the concerned look in his eyes had me going. We walked side by side out the front entrance. That's when it hit me—maybe it was Carolina. She had seen me go into the bathroom, and she was definitely obsessed with Jason. But I wasn't the reason Jason wasn't into her.

"Oh, in English this girl, Cathy, you know her?" he asked.

"No," I said.

"She told me that the final is going to be on this poem. I thought you might want a heads up. You have the same class behind me, right?"

Funny, he said he wasn't a stalker, but he knew a little too much about my schedule. "I guess," I said.

He pulled out a wrinkle-free photocopy from his backpack. "'The Road Not Taken' by Frost. It's supposed to be on the first half of the final."

"I know the poem." I pushed the poem away. I figured it was his original. To confess, a tiny part of me was struck by the fact that he took AP English.

"This is an extra copy I made. You can keep it," he said.

"Can I really?" I said. I meant to be sarcastic, but I don't know if he caught that.

For the next hour and a half, I brainstormed, he took immaculate notes, and we both researched. I tried my best to play it cool even when his hand occasionally touched mine for no reason at all—if you call reaching for the same magazine at the same time no reason. Usually, my personal wall was like the Great Wall of China. I wasn't sure if he liked me or didn't like me. I had no idea how to act, so I acted platonic ... way platonic.

"So what's the deal with the chess set?" he asked.

"You play?" I asked.

He laughed.

I remember so well because his smile for a moment felt like it was just for me.

"You?" He asked.

"Yeah, I've been known to win a few games," I said.

He leaned in so close to me I could smell his cologne.

"You want to?" he asked.

I leaned back just enough not to be sucked into his puppy dog eyes. "There's a game going on." I wasn't sure how to put it without sounding strange, yet at this point I figured he already thought that.

"My mom and I keep a game going. We usually move our pieces while the other person is doing something else."

"Why?"

"It's our thing."

He shook his head in agreement. "I used to have a thing ... with a girl, not my parents."

"You're the one that asked me to play. You say that as if

you're the one slumming? I have a 3.7 GPA so, yeah, maybe I don't have a boyfriend, but I invited you to my house. How dare you say that to me?" I could see the wheels in his head turning. He was insulted, as he should've been.

"I'm going to go," he said.

"I think that's a good idea," I said.

He packed his books and walked to the door.

I walked several steps behind him. I could feel my heart rate drop. Before he opened the door he turned to me quickly. For a second I lost my breath. He grabbed my hand and pulled me to him. I put my hand on his chest. His heart was racing. Good. He was nervous too. Was he going to kiss me? Of course I waited like an idiot to find out, like I had no choice in the matter. He snagged a marker from his backpack and ripped the lid off with his teeth. He wrote on my hand. I looked down to read the ... word? Seemed like he was a writing an entire letter. I bit my lips to keep from laughing. It tickled a little.

SORRY is all he wrote. I looked up to find him staring at me, waiting for approval. I could feel myself becoming flushed. Every bone in my body wanted to slam him against the door and kiss the heck out him. Instead I grabbed his arm.

"It's okay. I overreacted."

He gave me the head nod. What did that mean? Was I feeling more out of my league than ever or what? He opened the door, and I let him walk out. On his way to the curb he turned around.

"So maybe I don't have a girlfriend," he said.

I tried my best not to show every tooth in my mouth. "Don't smile. Somebody might think you actually like me," he continued. I thought I was going to choke on my own saliva.

www.CameoTheNovel.com

I stood there on my porch in shock as he drove away in his red Mustang. I kept wondering what was next. My heart nearly jumped out of my chest. I took a deep breath and slammed the front door behind me.

I snagged my Undercover Starlet™ journal to tell somebody about my day. My journal was the only place I was sure a secret could be safe. Before I could put pen to paper my cell phone was ringing. I knew it could only be one of two people: my mom or Cindy. As I picked up the phone, I recalled the days when I had spent all afternoon text messaging girls I had just met at some party who became my fast friends. I was having popularity withdrawal, which I quickly snapped out of at the sound of my mother's high-pitched voice.

"Nia! Hello. I can't stay long, honey. I'm just calling to check in. Where are you?" she asked.

"Home," I said. That was smart. I should think before I speak sometimes.

"What!" There it was, more of the high-pitched, I'm-in-mortal-shock tone of voice. "I specifically told you, young lady, to go to your grandparents'."

I guess this wouldn't be the time to tell her I had already had a study appointment with Jason and couldn't break it. "Cindy is coming over right now. You said I could go to her house."

"I don't want to hear another word about this. When I call you after my next appointment you had better be at your grandparents'. You understand? Or your cell phone and your cable and your closet are off limits!"

The way she said "off limits" reminded me of one of those deep-voiced villains from those fantasy flicks. She sounded so omnipotent like if you didn't follow her orders, she would somehow know.

"Can I sleep at Cindy's tonight?"

There was a long silence.

"Mom, are you there?" I asked.

"Yes, I'm here. You can stay at Cindy's. But be there when I call, otherwise there's going to be a problem," she said.

"Yes," I said.

"I love you," she said. These were the moments where I challenged parental law. How could you love someone you wanted to completely dominate?

"Goodbye, Mom." I could hear her sigh on the other end right before I hung up.

The sun was about to set. And although I thought my mother was a little paranoid, there could be no pranks tonight or I would be dead meat. I could hear her telling my dad about how I disobeyed her and the house got toilet-papered or something. No one could know I was home alone. Unless Cindy told someone? Or if she invited some people over. That was so her M.O. I was torn between closing all the shades and dialing Cindy. Good thing I had voice dialing and speaker phone on my cell, so I could multitask.

"Cin, did you tell anyone my mom wasn't home?" I asked.

"Excuse me?" she asked.

"I know it's weird, but can you just answer the question?" I said.

"Whatever. Do you think of me as a blabbermouth? Because I so am not. I never told anybody about your crush on Jaden."

"You swore never to mention that. It wasn't a crush. It was

www.CameoTheNovel.com

a momentary lapse of judgment." Jaden was this super tall, geeky type of boy who was kind of annoying. Kids either liked him or hated him. All he did was crack jokes about people. He had liked me since junior year and, for like one day, in a desperate, post-Craig moment, I had thought I liked him. After I thought about telling him, I realized I found him annoying. He was too silly and immature. What reasonable boy blows spit balls and pranks people with whoopee cushions?

"Whatever. I can't let your cloud of negativity get me down because I have some rad news." Occasionally, Cindy took a trip to the valley to learn "slang." I went to the front windows to close the curtains. That's when I saw this girl standing by a tree across the street. She took out a mirror and shined a reflection of the sun into the window.

"Okay, Cin, tell me when you see me. Bye." I hung up abruptly. I moved to the windows in the dining room. She was there, but she was on the other side of the tree with that same mirror, now reflecting the sun into the dining room window. What was she doing? Trying to burn a hole in the glass? She turned around. I had to admit those big Jackie O–style glasses were to die for. But what the heck was she doing standing on the street dressed to the nines? She waved at me, and I quickly shut the curtains. This was not good. This was so not good.

The doorbell rang. My breathing became intense like when I thought you-know-who was going to you-know-what me on the lips (I'm trying to block that memory of him, with hopes of this not turning into a full-blown crush). I slowly looked through the peep hole. Nothing! No one was there. I thought of pressing the panic button on the alarm. I ripped the cordless phone base out from the wall in the living room to use as a weapon. The bell rang again. Then my cell phone started to

www.UndercoverStarlet.com

ring. So this creep had my cell phone number.

I lifted the cordless phone and heavy base over my head and swung the door open. I jumped out. And there was Cindy standing at the door dressed in a white skirt and a shirt like the girl across the street.

"What are you doing? Trying to give me a heart attack?" I yelled.

"Excuse me? Do not go ballistic on me. I had to walk here. See, my dad let his car run out of oil. His engine has some problems, so he confiscated my car to run that one into the ground as well," she explained.

Although it sounded real brutal and all, I had bigger problems. "Get inside quick." I searched the street to see if anyone was watching. Something was coming. I could feel it. "Were you standing across the street?"

"Whatever, I just got here."

"That's not what I asked."

"Shouldn't I ask you why you are holding the phone over your head?"

"You tell me. If you're part of some prank, you better tell me now. I hate weird surprises. I am not kidding. I will not speak to you again if you ..."

"Are you threatening not to speak to me? I've told you things not even my mother knows. She thinks she's my best friend. I'm practically betraying her by telling you."

"Talk about shallow."

"I'm not shallow," Cindy said.

"Right," I said.

"You talk a real good game, Nia, but you're acting pretty

www.CameoTheNovel.com

shady. I don't know anything about a prank. What do I look like? If it doesn't involve a fine guy, I'm not wasting my extracurricular time on it. Any best friend of mine would know that!" she said.

"I knew it. The poem, the bodyguard act, the hand holding, Jason liking me all of a sudden is some kind of hoax."

"Jason likes you?"

"Don't change the subject. Someone is punking me."

"Why would somebody do that?"

"Are you wearing a hat?"

"Um, by the lack of one on my head, I'd have to go with no on that one." Cindy was the only person I knew who was more sarcastic than I was.

"Are you sure?" I asked.

She rolled her eyes at me. "I'm not punking you. Get that in your head. And I'm appalled that you think I would do something like that to you without telling you about it."

I plopped down on the couch and threw my head into my hands. "What if it's Carolina?" I said.

"Hmmm. What is she doing to you exactly?" Cindy asked.

I nervously flipped my hair around. Just the thought of Carolina having any power over me made my blood boil. I didn't even know if she had the brains to do something like this. "I slipped on some Kool-Aid in the bathroom while someone held the door shut right before lunch."

"What! Who even touches Kool-Aid! That is so '80s. Besides the fact that it doesn't have any vitamins. No wonder she's gross. She's malnourished," Cindy said.

"Oh, gosh!" I said.

www.UndercoverStarlet.com

"Then again, she doesn't have the wherewithal to put something like this together. It's too complicated for her. Look how basic her insults are," Cindy said.

"Since when did we start measuring intelligence by the intricacy of one's insults?"

"FYI, she couldn't get Jason to do anything. Especially not fake-like you. Nia and Jason sitting in a tree, k-i-s-s-i-n-g," Cindy added.

If she only knew the half of it. "There will be none of that."

"There might be if he shows up to the party tonight."

"I knew it!" I shouted.

"Who told you?" she asked.

I was careful not to accuse Cindy. This time she was going to admit it. "A little birdie."

"So you want to go?"

"Well, how could I not go?" Especially if it was going to be at my house.

"You're not wearing that, are you?"

"Maybe. You're not expecting me to play hostess, are you?" I couldn't believe I was entertaining this.

"You're not making any sense. Peter is hosting. I fully intend on being with Peter the whole night, but not as a hostess."

"I have to stay over your house tonight."

"It's cool. Just make sure you don't dress like that."

We made our way up to my bedroom. "Turn on the hallway light," I said. "Why are you so scary about everything?" she asked.

"Look, I said I was never going to go to any of these popular circuit parties again. If there's anything to be scared about, it's that!"

"Just think of it as a favor to Jason."

"And will Roger be there?"

"Don't go there."

"I think he's sort of eccentric. I mean he's nice," I said.

"Yuck! He's like a techie," she said.

"Appearances can be deceiving. I'm learning. He could be some undercover hottie," I said.

Cindy burst into laughter. I sifted through my segregated closet. One side was sexy, with my boyfriend-type gear, and the other side was I'm-cute-in-my-skinny-jeans-and-fitted-sweatshirt type of gear. I wore the sweatshirt-type gear nearly everyday.

"No jeans, lover girl. It's all about the dress. Fluffy at the bottom to leave something to the imagination and super tight at the top. I say that if you can bounce a quarter off your belly, you got to show it off. It's all about the waist!" Cindy said.

She wanted to be a fashion editor at a teen magazine. Her sole purpose in life was to tell people how to dress for the season. I pulled out a hot black dress I had worn out with Craig once for our two-week anniversary.

"I'm in."

I wanted to see Jason's face when he saw me in that dress. Though I hadn't forgotten how he hadn't called me that summer. It felt like I was holding on more than remembering. Hadn't he apologized? Too bad. I couldn't just unleash myself and throw myself into his arms.

Chapter 6

"You are so kidding me," Cindy said.

"No, I would never kid about gossip, cross my heart and hope to die. Peter smiled when he found out that you said you were coming. It is a must hook-up," Jane said.

"PG, of course … for tonight, maybe," Cindy said, as if she had actually thought about how far she would go. They called Cindy and Jane the Gossip Mafia. Jane had better intelligence sources than the CIA, and Cindy always got the word on corroborating evidence to support Jane's gossip.

They had met in freshman year when they had both tried out for the school drill team, until they realized that the team did not practice anywhere near the basketball team. Add to that the fact that practice was a grueling three hours each day with social bottom feeders as the boy assistants to the team. It was more than enough to make them ditch the tryouts. They clicked instantly, Cindy says. Me? I was just an innocent bystander—a friend, if you will. When I hung with them it was less of the Nia show and more of the circuit news. I used to love it when I dated a boy who was hot on the circuit, but now I was just an observer. People just started calling them the Gossip Mafia. It could've been because that's how they signed the original morning text messages: BY GOSSIP MAFIA.

Anyone who was anyone in school got the morning gossip text, and all you did was pray your name wasn't in it. Of course, anyone who replied back to retaliate against any of the accusations of lust and betrayal would only incite more flagrant news about them the following morning and their phone number would somehow get deleted from the forward list. Eventually, word spread not to respond when you received the gossip text, as it could never result in anything pleasant. Jane was sweet, though. She was the type of clever girl who never bought the shirt she tried on at a store. She always put that one back and got a new one in the same size to take home. She was the only person I knew who had an official jaywalking strategy. She only stood off the curb when attempting to jaywalk if she was standing behind someone else who took all the risk out of getting hit if a car jumped the curb because they were in front. Whoever heard of a jaywalking strategy? Jane was creative.

"Thanks again, Jane, for the blended latte!" I said.

"Oh, no worries. You're gonna need it if this is your first rendezvous on a weeknight since ..." Jane said.

She looked at Cindy and whispered, "Is it cool to mention his name now or are we still all mum's the word since, you know, the Craig thing?"

Cindy looked at me. I shrugged like it was cool. Cindy tried to inconspicuously nod her head to tip Jane off.

"Great! This brings me to my latest and greatest piece of meat," Jane said.

Cindy gasped. Were they drama queens or what?

"So, the word is ..." Jane paused to take a sip of her latte. Cindy and I waited in anticipation. "Michelle wants to break up with Craig."

"No! She was just bragging about him in our section of the hall. Where did you get your info?" Cindy asked.

"Swear not to tell anyone," Jane said.

Cindy looked at me, and I knew she would swear not to tell anyone but she would dare to tell everyone. That was kind of their thing. They liked to pretend that the gossip was sacred, but we all knew Jane would begin texting that to everyone in the morning.

"Swear," Cindy said.

"Lucy was whispering it to someone in the D3 bathroom," Jane said.

D3 was, like, this half floor where the girls' gym class was.

"Check it. We're about to roll up to this party in an over-priced foreign sports utility vehicle, dressed like supermodels," Cindy said.

"I'm poised for a comeback," I said.

"In that outfit? I'd say it's going to be epic," Cindy said.

I took a deep breath. I hoped I was ready for this. Jane jammed the breaks on her SUV in front of the house. My mouth dropped open maybe two nanoseconds before Cindy's.

"What is she doing?" Cindy was as serious as a high school senior being interviewed for the college of her dreams, though even then she probably wouldn't have sounded so direct.

Cindy jumped out of the car as if it were on fire. She marched up to Carolina, who was holding Jason's hand. I, on the other hand, acted as if I had not even seen them. I didn't know what this had to do with my incidents, but I didn't want to look directly in her eyes without knowing what I was going to say. It took me a second or two, and then I had it.

Cindy stopped in her tracks. She surveyed Carolina's outfit. "I see last season's pink, last year's poplin shirt, and an in-season belt with matching shoes. I get it. You, Jason, must be ushering her to the Secret Fashion Victim's page photo-op. Did I mention I voted you in for that page, Carolina?" Cindy had joined the yearbook committee to even the playing field. Some of her enemies would go down in high school history as the worst dressed, least liked, most likely to be single forever, and best class kiss-up.

"Jealousy is such an ugly color on you," Carolina said.

"Whatever. I don't look ugly in anything. You should know. Seems like I had those shoes on last week. Of course they looked like showstoppers on my feet, but on your feet they look like bargain basement pumps!" Cindy said.

I would've questioned Carolina if I thought I would get a straight answer out of her. If that ridiculous jealousy comment showed me anything, she was definitely not smart enough to be operating alone.

Since when is jealousy a color? Though she was hand in hand with someone who could be the enemy in disguise. He was steadily disarming me with his charms. How clever! I couldn't keep my eyes off him for a second.

"Nia, hi," he said.

I passed him by without so much as a smile. My eyes told of my disapproval and suspicion. Or, at least, I thought they did. It's like you always think you're giving signals to guys but you never really know how they'll interpret them.

Next thing I knew, his hand was on my arm pulling me back to him. He had let go of Carolina's hand to come question me.

"Now that you're fancy, you don't know me?" Before I could answer, he put his lips to my ear. "You play a good game, but you're still not at checkmate. I'm feelin' the dress, pretty lady," he said.

www.UndercoverStarlet.com

"Do you like the dress?"

My black stretch, strapless cotton dress that ended just about three inches above my knees was doing its job then. So he thought this was like playing a game of chess. And what would've been the prize if I won? Him? I leaned close to his face and rocked my head slightly to the left then the right as if I was looking for the best way to kiss him. If he was going to go all romantic comedy on me, I had to step up to the plate. Then, just when he leaned into me, I turned my face and let him kiss my cheek.

"You can look, but you can't touch. You might be at check, but you haven't won the game yet." I turned on my heel, knowing he would watch me all the way to the door. Who was running the pranks now? As soon as I hit the door, I remembered just how obnoxiously loud these parties could be. My ears would be ringing for days thanks to the huge speakers bumping club tracks with mad bass.

I turned to the shamelessly enormous great room, I think that's what these folks call their second living rooms these days—or at least that's what my mom says. Inside the great room, every girl within 100 feet looked at me out of the corner of her eye and whispered something to the girl next to her. This bunch was discreet. I spotted Cindy sitting on Peter's lap, laughing loudly near the picturesque ocean view. She was cuddling him close; for a second they looked like a couple.

She always knew what to do to get a guy eating out of the palm of her hand. And, with her, there was never a moment wasted. It was an exact science. Every move was calculated down to the way she threw her hand across his chest as she laughed at his jokes. Watching Cindy was like getting a lesson in Flirting 101. Anyway, the lesson was over. It was time for me to circulate.

On my way to the punch bowl in the dining room, I passed Lucy and Michelle. By the time I spotted those two hags, I was already on their radar.

"Who cleaned that old dog up?" Lucy asked Michelle.

I was surprised she even had her own lowly insults to throw. For the most part, it seemed like they shared a brain. But lo and behold, this was evidence that Lucy might actually be able to come up with her own thoughts.

"I don't know whether to pet you or give you a treat. Wait, that would be your owner's job. She's all yours, Michelle," I said.

Michelle studied my face intently, hoping that on some freak chance I might submit to her nonverbal aggression. I guess someone told her she was intimidating. Please! I flipped my loosely curled hair over my shoulder and into her face.

Where there was Michelle, Craig wasn't far behind. There he was, carrying—better yet, juggling—two of every drink available. What were they doing? Using him for a taste test. He tried to make eye contact with me. Just to mess with him, I purposely didn't look at him while I walked toward him. And, well, my foot might have mistakenly interrupted his path.

"Timber!" I yelled. With the high, cathedral ceilings in that place, my voice echoed. Everyone in the dining room couldn't take their eyes off Craig. It was good to have someone else feeling the heat for once. I got a little ginger ale on my leg. It was a small price to pay considering Craig's fresh white tee was now an array of wet, patchy fruit juice colors.

I bent down to wipe off my leg. I overheard a girl from my gym class talking to another girl. "Yeah, she's outside with him now. They've been gone for like twenty minutes," she said.

"Oh, there he is. Do you think they, you know?" the other girl asked.

"Whatever happened to saving something for prom night?" the girl from gym class said. Apparently the girl from gym class was ticked off. I waited to see if the two girls were going to walk away so I could see who they were talking about. About sixty seconds passed before I realized that I didn't have all day. So I decided to show my face. They took one look at me and cleared out. If I would've known that, I would've saved myself a wasted minute.

Just then, I started to feel the burn of my three-inch stilettos. What I would've given for a pair of sneakers.

"I didn't know you'd be here," Jason said.

"Maybe you should pretend I'm not," I said. What if they were talking about ... ? "Jason! Don't grab me like that." I couldn't even complete a thought with this guy around. He leaned in close to me from behind with his arm around my neck. It was much less of a grab and much more of a hold that he had on me. It had been so long I couldn't tell the difference.

"Let me know when we get to checkmate," he whispered in my ear.

I took a deep breath and began to cough. I removed his arm from my neck. There was no telling where it had been. "Try again when you don't reek of fragrance."

I only knew one girl who bathed in Undercover Starlet™ fragrance as if it were lotion for a dry skin problem. How dare he think he could play me that? "I actually started to believe that ..." I laughed uneasily. "Give my regards to Carolina. No hard feelings. I'll consider this thing a cameo." I shrugged it off and walked away.

"Nia," he called out under his breath.

I pretended I didn't hear him. My body must have agreed with me too, because all of a sudden I found myself bouncing to the beat of the new song "Cameo." The DJ must have been reading my mind.

He tapped me from behind. I was walking upstairs to retreat to the bathroom to do the usual—every party I did the same thing. I spent ten minutes in the bathroom, looking at myself in the mirror and wondering why I was even at the party. I guess I could face him first, no?

"Seems they're playing our song," I said.

"What? Why do you say that?"

"We're not really meant to be. I think you've found yourself a girlfriend," I said.

"You think too much. She asked me to help her with her car. It wouldn't start or something."

"Her car? Right! Did you give her a tune-up? I bet you checked under the hood." Was I really pretending to be jealous of Carolina?

"Okay. She kissed me, but I told her I was talking to someone." He said that last part under his breath.

"We don't have to talk about this. You could have any girl here. So, this is my shadow leaving the place." I walked away from him, knowing he was probably telling the truth. I turned to him and sang, "I guess you understand why we can't be. Thought it over and this is what came to me. You're my cameo lover. No need for another." I blew him a kiss.

A few minutes later, my out-of-use cell phone had received its first text message all day.

I opened the message: "Game on. Your cameo lover."

www.UndercoverStarlet.com

I checked the sender, and it was private. This was the second private message I had gotten this week. I didn't even have Jason's number saved. I was confused. Jason didn't really seem to be secretive like this—he seemed like he would sign his name. Maybe I was just reading too much into this.

One month without a boyfriend, and I didn't know how to flirt. Yet, then again, when did flirting become borderline menacing? And there was still the question of who pulled the bathroom stunt. Who would work with Carolina and what would they get out of it? She was kind of pretty, but there was something about her that reminded me of a rat. I did once hear that her stepdad was loaded and that she had bribed her first boyfriend into staying with her an extra month by buying him a new pair of sneakers. Obviously she was about as deep as a puddle, so I could only imagine the type of guy that would fathom dating her.

I looked around the hallway inconspicuously. The farther down the hallway I went, this place felt more and more like one of those eerie fun houses. Did they have me on camera or something? My face was probably glaring with oil. Years ago, during a bout with acne I had used this infomercial stuff that was like steroids in a bottle, and since halting all use of that skin kit thing, my skin was like an oil slick two or three hours after washing my face. Better on the surface than in my pores, is what I told myself. But on camera, with a few editing tricks, I could quickly go from fresh-faced and dewy to greasy and gooey.

A frantic panic came over me. I asked some random girl in the hallway where the bathroom was. She pointed all the way to the end of the hall. Suddenly it seemed like I had been walking forever. That was when I stumbled upon Cindy and Peter.

www.CameoTheNovel.com

Oh, gosh! I couldn't stop staring. It was so rude. They didn't seem to notice me between Peter taking off Cindy's cardigan, and Cindy wrapping her legs around him like he was the dreaded rope climb in gym class. She told me that she always wore layers to parties for this exact purpose—as she put it, guys liked to rip your clothes off, so a girl had to build up the anticipation by having more to take off. He clumsily opened the door and the two stumbled into his bedroom. I took a step forward, allowing my eyes to follow them in. They dropped to the floor about three feet shy of his huge king-size bed. His room was decorated like one of those sleek, modern hotel rooms with a brown suede headboard and dark blue curtains and sheets, and there was even a sofa and a fifty- or sixty-inch flat-screen. Yet there were no pictures on the walls or anything. A few soccer trophies, some staged lacrosse racquets ... I guess that's what you called them. I didn't know what the game entailed, but I did know that lacrosse had been invented by Native Americans. Why was I thinking of this at a party? Probably because I'd rather be at home reading a book. In short, the room was nice but stale.

I felt relieved that I didn't live in one of these humongous farm houses with so much space one wouldn't know what to do with it. But the decorating was lovely. That was my mother's word: lovely. I continued down the hallway in search of a bathroom.

I knew Cindy was promiscuous. But she was my best friend. I looked at her as being in control of her dating life rather than submitting to pressure or doing it to be liked. She had a lot of strengths that made her really cool. Seeing her in action had me in shock, though. I just kept thinking that she barely knew him. It was, like, yesterday when he gave her his number. I wasn't one to sleep with every guy I fancied. In fact, I had only slept with one guy in my entire life.

"Entire life" is such a weighted phrase. Here's my disclaimer—I'd only reached puberty at age fourteen, and I believed a girl shouldn't have sex before seventeen. That was the magic number of maturity in my book. Although my friends said most girls lost it at sixteen.

This was not the time for a soliloquy. There wasn't a line at the bathroom, surprise surprise.

At these types of shindigs, there was always a long wait to use the restroom. It was beautiful, the bathroom. It had honed marble countertops, beautifully marble tiled floors, a steam shower, and a classic view of the ocean, though I guess anybody out in the ocean had a classic view of me too. Now this was definitely the type of bathroom I wanted to have built right next to my bedroom. I did the obligatory makeup check. I was so paranoid about people being able to see me that I turned out the light. I could still see with the moonlight.

After I used the swanky toilet, I realized there was a shadow of an animal on the floor right in front of the sink. It was either a bird or a squirrel—probably a bird, because it didn't have a tail from what I could see. The large window wrapped around the corner, so I peeked my head around the corner. Just how big was this bathroom? I found a complete mirror, vanity, and a huge spa tub. This bathroom was almost as big as the entire second floor of my house. Then I spotted the red cardinal perched on the window seat. That was weird. As long as he was alive, I was still safe. Dead birds were always harbingers of bad things to come. Before I turned to wash my hands the red bird dropped off the cliff as if his wings had malfunctioned. If I wasn't such a germaphobe, I would've turned on the lights to ease my anxiety. But I hadn't washed my hands yet, and I hated spreading germs—which reminded me, the doorknob was probably full of germs anyway.

www.CameoTheNovel.com

I finally washed and dried my hands. I used the same paper towel I dried my hands with to twist the door knob. That's when I realized this gold body glow stuff Cindy insisted I put on was all uneven. One spot looked like I had doused a whole bottle of the stuff on it. I could've skipped cleaning it off with a paper towel and hand soap, but I did it anyway.

Oddly, I could see two dusty, black tennis shoes standing right behind me.

Someone slapped a hand across my mouth. I stomped my foot on theirs. Then I yanked at the hand on my mouth. I looked at myself in the oversize mirror. And it freaked me out even more. Was this me under siege? This was like a bad action movie with me as the victim. How did I get here? The skinny arms were one clue. But once I shifted my focus from me, I realized the person was wearing mascara. Unless he was gay, this was a girl. I dug my nails into her arm. Oodles of anger and fear ripped through my veins. Who did she think she was? She looked skinny, but her grip on my face was insane. I kept pulling at her hand to get it off. I wasn't about to be ambushed by some cross-dressing stalker. If this was a representation of good and evil the line was clear.

"Listen, don't scream."

I tried to open my mouth to bite her hand, but it was a failed attempt. The pressure she had on my mouth prevented my lips from moving enough for me to bite. Then she tightened her grip on my jaw. I elbowed her in the stomach. That was the only thing I could remember from self-defense day in gym class. All year long, they teach you how to play volleyball, yet only one day was dedicated to what turned out to be most useful.

"Dang," she said. She let go of my mouth.

I wailed, "Help!"

Suddenly it felt like a brick was being smashed against my intestines. My cries for help had dried up. I had been silenced by a karate chop in the stomach. Next thing I knew, she swung her foot underneath mine. I flew to the ground. You would've thought she had taken my self-defense class. I knew that move, so why didn't I use it?

"I am here to help you."

If I wasn't ready to unload whatever drops were left in my bladder before those words, I was definitely ready to do so after them.

"Stay down, insolent. I am not trying to assault you."

"You wouldn't assault me."

I grabbed her ankle and yanked it toward me.

"Ahhh!" she screamed. Then she hit the floor with a loud thud. I reached for the door.

"I'm a whistleblower, if I may," she said. She quickly jumped up and slammed the door. What was she, an acrobat?

"The time has come to blow the whistle," she said. She sounded like a cross between a cheesy proverb and a fortune cookie.

"Come ON!" I threw my forearm into her stomach. That knocked her back a few paces. I opened the door again. "Help!" I yelled.

She slammed the door again.

"If you're here to help, then why don't you stay down?" I grabbed hold of her throat with my tightest grip. I didn't know what had come over me. What was she doing walking into a locked bathroom dressed like a robber in a dark ski mask, oversize overalls, and black leather gloves?

"Get off me!" She dug her fingernails into my hand. Though she had gloves on, it felt like they were piercing my skin.

"No! Why don't you blow the whistle and do what you came here to do?" I asked.

"As if I had any concern with beating you up. There are worse things, many of which have already happened to you. Now I only asked you to move your hand to give you a chance to get on my good side."

I let go of her neck a little. I mean, I didn't intend to strangle her. This was getting a little too violent. She quickly pushed me into the door, grabbed my leg, and twisted it. Next thing I knew, I had flown off balance and landed face-down right into the floor.

"I'm a purple belt in karate! I'm going to tell you this in the hopes that you spread the word." She laughed. "Should you share this with anyone you will find yourself blacked out of the yearbook like you never existed. There are those of us who prefer it that way."

I tried to push myself off the ground only to be pinned down by her narrow foot.

"This started out as a freshman prank. An initiation into our house, if you will. But there is one who has taken this too far. She has watched you closely and has much to vindicate. She has heard you sing, as you might be aware. This is a warning. We are no longer involved in this."

"And what does your house represent?"

"You will tell no one of this if you wish to be acknowledged as a part of the student body," she said.

"Who heads this club?" I asked.

"You do not ask questions of me!" she said.

There was a knock at the door.

"Come in," I yelled.

"You're so stupid."

The person opened the door, and she shut it. "Do not come in. I am not dressed," she said. Suddenly the light went out. Then she threw the door back. It slammed into my already pulsating foot that was jammed into a three-inch stiletto pump. I heard her run expediently down the hall. Then I heard a slam just outside the door.

"Say excuse me!"

It was Jane's voice. After peeling myself off the floor, I rushed out the door.

"What are you doing in there?" Jane asked.

I wasn't sure if the yearbook thing was serious, but I very well couldn't tell the gossip mill herself what was going on.

"Ohh ... I was using the vanity in the back, while she used the mirror. Makeup check."

"What is that mark on your face?"

"What?" I touched my face to find a crease on my cheek. "Do you have a compact?" I asked. Jane and I walked down the hall.

"Did you see that girl?" I had to be clever. A gossip queen never resisted an opportunity to talk about someone.

"Who?" Jane asked.

Get a clue. "The girl who just ran out of the bathroom," I said.

"Dude, what was with that hot black turtleneck? It's ninety degrees outside. Is this or is this not a party? Hello? She was totally uninvited. I can so tell. Nobody invited would dress like that," Jane said.

"What was with her hair color?" I said fishing for details. I didn't get a chance to see her without the mask on. I wondered if Jane had noticed her hair.

"She needed a gloss, and some auburn highlights. That mousy brown look is so junior high, as if anyone has virgin hair these days."

So we had a match for the black turtleneck from the bedroom incident and this one involved a mask.

Jane handed me the compact. Yeah, it was as I had suspected. I had a tile imprint on my cheek. If I thought the door knob was dirty, every germ on every shoe that had entered that bathroom was now residing on my face.

"I have to go home."

"I get it. You've made the rounds. Talked to Jason and all."

I stopped dead in my tracks. Jane kept walking about ten feet before she realized I had deferred.

"What?" She looked back at me confused.

"We are not seeing each other. No. Not even close." I had to make that clear, otherwise I'd be in the morning text report. The day Craig and I had broken up I didn't receive the morning text. Probably because my name was all over it. It turns out I had mysteriously been deleted from the send list. Cindy made sure to put me back on.

We reached the top of the stairs. Carolina brushed past us. She only dreamed of appearing in the morning report. "The second bathroom on this floor stinks of D-list trash," Carolina said.

"I'd be careful who I called D-list," Jane said.

I just ignored Carolina. It was beyond my patience level. Though one thing was weird. Why was she referring to the second bathroom? She didn't really have mousy brown hair. But it could've been a wig. Was she part of the "house" that crazy Taekwondo Girl from the bathroom represented? Taekwondo girl knew the same moves from gym class. We must've had gym together. I had gym with Carolina. But, then again, so did fifty-nine other girls.

I had a feeling that this had something to do with the very group of people I despised—the popular clique. So this "house" was made up of girls? I wondered if Jane was a member. I guess she had to be to have such a strong hold on the tabloid media. It would be weird if guys weren't members.

"I'm going to look for Cindy," Jane said.

"I think she's upstairs with Peter." I cleared my throat.

"Oh." Jane shook her head. Then she checked her watch. "I give them five minutes," Jane said.

"That sounds about right," I said.

We both looked at each other and laughed.

The thing that got to me was that boys had the power to make a girl popular. I was a living specimen of that. So, if guys were members, why would they send a girl to rough me up? Popularity controlled by a secret society. This whole notion was completely absurd. You couldn't be a member if you weren't popular? Yet, you could be popular and not be a member? Uh! Look at me, I was thinking on their shallow level. This was supposed to be all behind me.

www.CameoTheNovel.com

I texted Cindy to meet us at the car and copied Jane. I walked out the door to get some fresh air. It felt like I should tell someone, but I didn't know who that girl was or if she would be back. And this other person she spoke of ... It had sounded like she was insinuating that something was looming. What could be next? My mind was racing a mile a minute. I couldn't even complete a thought. That bathroom incident was downright jarring. I didn't even know what to call it, but there would be another like it I suspected. How could I stop it? Was this the type of thing you reported to the dean? What would they do? Sequester every brown-haired girl to the dean's office for questioning? I hadn't really been in a brawl since grade school. And at least then I knew who I was fighting and why they hated me.

Jason rolled by in his convertible with the top down. He nodded at me and smiled. Then, when I didn't respond, he waved. I see you. I smiled and quickly looked away. You can never give a guy too much of your attention, that's when things start to go south. I'm a living specimen of that, too. Plus, I was beginning to think that if I cut him loose this might be all over. How could I ever use the bathroom again without getting freaked out after this? I tried not to let the first incident give me a complex, but this would be difficult to let go.

Chapter 7

The next morning, Cindy and I bummed a ride to school with her father.

"I'm so sorry about this," Cindy said.

"What?"

"Uh, this whole carpool thing. Having to listen to my father's lame jokes. I keep telling him he's not funny, but he swears my friends think he is."

Although her dad's jokes were pretty dry, we only had to endure them for ten minutes on our way to school. It was no problem, really. Dealing with the car ride trumped spending my nights at the all-you-can-eat with my grandparents and sleeping in the guest bedroom that reeked of mothballs.

"So I shouldn't laugh anymore?" I asked.

"No," Cindy said firmly. "Looks like you got company."

Jason was waiting for me at the front entrance. I had totally forgotten about the whole chaperone thing. I should've been down on my knees, thanking my lucky stars for some backup. I hadn't told anyone about last night. And I wasn't planning on it.

"He's looking at you. Wait a minute? Is he waiting to walk you to class? Aw!" Cindy said in a mocking girly voice.

"And where's Peter? Oh ... you've got no strings attached. I'm sure there's a girl *somewhere* who envies you."

Cindy's mouth dropped. I didn't usually talk to her like that. But she was getting on my nerves a little, with her watching every move that Jason and I made.

"That was way harsh. BTW, keep this up and you'll be in the morning spiel for the next week, Missy." Cindy winked.

"And maybe I could use a little heat my way," I said.

She knew I was being facetious. I hoped.

Jason stared me down as I approached him. I acted as if I hadn't spotted him fifteen feet away. I let Cindy walk in front of me a bit as I slowed my pace. I looked at him and smiled coyly as I passed him by. He was cute all right—dark black hair, chocolate skin, big, brown, puppy dog eyes, tall, sort of built, definitely not skinny. Why did I keep describing him in my head over and over again? It's like I forgot how cute he is. I call it the "I like you amnesia"—you forget how he looks because you like him so much.

He casually looked around before practically tripping over himself to catch up with me. He covertly tugged at my arm. "Wait up," he said.

He was a persistent one.

"Hi," I said, like I had no idea he'd been trailing me. "Do you have a job, like a part-time job?" I asked him. If a boy had a part-time job, there was always a chance he had a girlfriend at work.

"Are you running a background check?" he asked as he followed me up the stairs. We had the same homeroom.

"You're the one creeping up from behind. It's plausible that some background would be in order." I had to think up that one.

"Just crush the ego, why don't you?" His tone changed from

www.UndercoverStarlet.com

charming and inquisitive to cold and dry. Note to self: Don't call him out on his fawning. I liked it better when he played charming.

"So … we're going to class?" he asked. He avoided direct eye contact with me. He walked ahead a little and held the stairwell door open for me.

"Why? Are you trying to weasel out?" I walked through the door. "Thanks," I said.

"Me? You know you're not like any other girl. For real."

I stopped in the middle of the hallway. "Is that a good thing?"

"You tell me." He shrugged.

This guy was everything I had sworn off. He grabbed my hand and led me up the hallway. The whole time I kept my palm open, refusing to grab back. It was so sudden that I didn't have any time to think. He had some game, though.

Then I realized we were on the wrong floor. I snatched my hand back. "Jason, we're on the wrong floor."

"Yeah, we'll just take the staircase at the end."

Could it be that were holding hands on this floor because he didn't want anybody to see us? Not that I wanted anyone to see either, because this complicated things. I leaned into him so close I noticed the length of his eyelashes.

"I did want you to take me to class, but now I'm walking alone." I couldn't believe it came out like that. I was supposed to say something witty, not petty. Goodness! I turned on my trusty stiletto heel—yeah, the same heel from the night before. I suspected that by third period my foot would probably start throbbing from the lack of blood circulation to my toes, but it would be a damn good-looking throbbing foot. The shoes

www.CameoTheNovel.com

were Cindy's. Since I'd been blacklisted socially, I'd rarely worn ridiculously high heels. Sometimes you have to change it up a little.

I hoped Jason got a mouth full of my hair back there when I turned around and bolted in the opposite direction. Was he attempting to take me to class the back way or what? He may be good-looking, but I was equally as hot! And I was smart. I knew the world was fixated on looks, but having a brain counted big time in my book.

"I am walking you to class. What's the deal?" he asked.

"What is *your* deal?" I said furiously.

He didn't answer me.

"Don't follow me," I continued.

The bell rang. In all the four years I'd been at this school, the bell had never come in handy until lately, although I'd never been late to homeroom before, until today.

I ran down the hallway and up the proper staircase. He ran after me. I could hear his colossal footsteps gaining speed. I had only one more flight to go. Everything would be fine as long as I didn't trip. These shoes were tricky. You could only let the base of your foot touch the step—not the high heel part. Otherwise you could definitely fall backward. By the time I reached the top of the second flight of stairs, I was winded. I stopped to take a breath. I mean, I was late already, no biggie. Wrong! There was a major biggie!

He grabbed me by the waist from behind, knocking me off balance. I jerked backward and then swayed forward in an effort to regain my balance and that I did. I snatched his hands off me.

"Nia! Are you okay?" Jason asked.

www.UndercoverStarlet.com

I caught a glimpse of him bolting up the stairs out of the corner of my eye. If he was running up the stairs, then who was grabbing on me? I turned completely around to find Craig standing behind me.

"What are you doing?" I slapped Craig across his face. "Don't touch me."

"What you doin', man?" Jason asked Craig.

"I thought you were right behind me," I said to Jason.

"Nah, I stopped chasing you after the first flight of stairs," Jason said.

"Why are you following her?" Craig sounded like a mechanical tin man. It took him three whole minutes to come up with that thought.

"I asked you a question, son," Jason said.

"This is none of your business," Craig said.

"I think it is." Jason stepped into Craig's face. I stepped in between them.

"Craig, why did you try to pull me down the stairs?" I asked.

Jason should've kicked his butt, but it wasn't worth it. He could get into a lot trouble. Our homeroom teacher was Mr. Sui. He was like Inspector Gadget. If you were late to class, he would contact someone on his BlackBerry and find out why you were late before you even made it into class.

"I was tryin' to whisper in your ear," Craig said to me loudly so Jason could hear.

"Nah, that's not going on," Jason said.

"Craig, I don't even talk to you. Take a hint. Leave me alone!" I walked away.

As soon as I turned my back, Craig pushed up against Jason. I opened the door and held it. When I looked behind me expecting to see Jason, I saw him all right. He had just shoved Craig into a wall five feet away. Craig charged at Jason. He motioned to grab Jason's neck. I quickly jumped in between them and put my hands up. The last thing I needed was anyone swinging their arms near me.

"Stop it, Craig. We are not going out anymore. You have a girlfriend! What are you doing?" I said.

"Can I talk to you?" Craig asked.

"No," I said.

Craig just stood there as if he hadn't realized that I wasn't waiting in the wings to take him back.

Now, somewhere between telling Craig off and leaving the stairwell, I had teleported out of my body, and a daring, flirty version of me grabbed Jason by the hand and walked to class confidently. We didn't look back at Craig. I knew he wasn't following us. In fact, for the first time in two days, I felt confident that no one was following us.

Our class was only one door from the staircase. The only door open was the front door. Walking through the front door sealed the deal. Everyone awake in homeroom was going to notice, and the rumor mill would start. Cindy's eyeballs stretched to the size of golf balls upon seeing us. I put one foot in the door with my hand in his. There were gasps. He was walking right behind me. Suddenly, I was summoned back to my body and, upon returning, I dropped Jason's hand and scurried to my seat embarrassed.

"What was that?" Cindy sounded impressed. I thought she was going to get out of her seat and bow down. Then again, knowing Cindy, she probably had thought of it.

"What?" I whispered innocently.

"No one has been able to lock that down all year. Do not screw this up with your scary, church-girl act like you're a saint or something. You came in looking all cool like this was finally your big comeback and then, at the last second, you punked out. Not cool."

I'm not sure why Mr. Sui felt compelled to read the morning handouts aloud to the entire class. The words, Graduation Check List, written in large red letters across the top like a warning letter ensured that we were all reading that announcement the moment it got into our hands. Some of us even looked over our neighbor's shoulder to read it if our neighbor snagged a copy before it came around to our row. There was change in the air. Cindy and I looked at each other, knowing the same thing was on both of our minds. She shook her head as if to say, "Yeah, it's coming."

"Graduation," I said.

"The big G. I'm just hoping for a new car," Cindy said.

I wondered what my hopes were for graduation besides putting all this menial popularity, "high school" stuff behind me and excelling based on my brains in college. I looked back at Jason, and he looked up from his graduation notice at me. I smiled. He smiled as his eyes dove back down to his paper. He was like no other boy I had ever met. Now I knew what that meant; it was a really good thing.

I turned back around to my lonely spiral notebook. I pulled out a little folded note that was peeking out right underneath the back cover. I waved the silly note in front of Cindy's face.

"I didn't know we'd turned the clock back to paper and pen," I said.

"I try to avoid using my notebook as often as possible. That did not come from me!" Cindy reached for the note. I pulled it back.

The last time she had gotten hold of a note written to me she read it aloud to the entire class. I quote: "Nia," she'd said like one of those overzealous beefcake men on the cover of a romance novel, with all this fake bass in her voice. "You look hot today. Pick you up after practice. Craig," she finished.

I had been mortified. Then the girl sitting next to me—note: I'd never spoken to her a day in my life—leaned over and said, "I would kill to be you right now." I'd always thought she was so smart. Then it hit me that everyone wanted a life, a boyfriend, and popularity. I was living the dream for every beautiful, smart girl like me. What a crock! That's the thing about epiphanies, they are highly contextually based. From the inside of the popularity group things seemed much different than from the outside looking in. I was almost ashamed at how gullible I had become. I was easily beguiled by my fake friends and my fake popular status. Many of those fake friends were in my same homeroom class. They watched me like a hawk when my back was turned. But if I glanced in their direction they'd put on a forced, uncomfortable half smile in an attempt to be civil. I didn't waste my time. I just looked right past them.

Anyway, to prevent another public offering of my private information, I slipped the note into my bra strap.

"Oh, no, you didn't!" Cindy said.

I snapped my finger in Cindy's face and said, "Don't act like you don't know."

Cindy and I both laughed.

"Shhh!" Mr. Sui said.

The morning announcements started on the PA system. In a

few moments, Cindy would become bored of this note and start to check her morning text messages—at least, that's what I was hoping for. Cindy had girlfriends who spilled their guts about their romp fests to her via text and guy friends who sent her offers for after-school dates via text. She had a busy inbox. There were some guys she liked and some guys that only wished she liked them. So most of those offers went unanswered, but they made good topics of conversation.

I quietly dragged the note from my bosom—as if! Anyway, the note said: "Check the basement at 4 p.m. They who wears a white hat and has taken from you that which they fear, you have re-gained only to shame them will make a Cameo."

I was sure this had been written by Taekwondo Girl. It was in her same proverb speech pattern. Weird. She must be in this homeroom. Cindy would know. I slipped the note in my back pants pocket.

"Listen, do you know anyone who speaks like a prophet?"

"No. Why?" Cindy asked.

I shrugged, and stood up. Homeroom was going to be over in 30 seconds. Jason started walking toward me when Cindy snatched the note from my back pocket.

"You should keep your jeans baggy if you don't want every crease or note imprint to show," Cindy said.

Jason and I stood in each other's presence without saying a word. I couldn't read what he was thinking.

"All right," I said.

I picked up my lone book and left, but not before grabbing the note back from Cindy. Jason followed behind me.

"What makes you think I didn't let you see that note?"

www.CameoTheNovel.com

I texted Cindy.

Jason and I continued down the hall, side by side, like an item.

"I hope you know I have no idea where we're going since I'm walking you to class," he said.

"I'll hold your hand to make sure you don't lose your way," I said.

"Make sure you want to," he said.

"Who gave you the note?" Cindy texted.

Unfortunately, I had to let go of his hand to text back. I knew he might not like that, but such is life. "Just on my desk. Ever heard of a popular society that initiates freshmen?" I texted.

"Where did you hear that?" she texted right back.

"Don't know," I texted.

"Want to check out?" she texted.

"Think I have to," I texted.

"What do you mean?" she texted.

"Will explain later," I texted. I put my phone away. Jason took my hand back.

I was trying to figure out what to say. "Here it is," I said.

I stopped just shy of the classroom door. As I faced him, I noticed something strange in my eye line. Right across from the classroom door was the word "Cameo" written in red lipstick. I tapped Jason on the shoulder. I couldn't take my eyes off the writing on the wall. This was downright peculiar.

"Do you see that, babe?"

First he looked at me strangely, and then he turned around to the wall. I couldn't believe I had the guts to call him "babe."

www.UndercoverStarlet.com

I could feel my heart fluttering.

"Why does it say 'Cameo'? Like that song?" he asked.

"I don't know."

The second bell rang, and that meant it was time to get to class.

"Guess she's found herself another sucker," Lucy said.

"Uh, ew-u. Why does every boy want to slum for her?" Michelle asked Lucy.

Jason looked at them angrily.

"She is such a creep," I said.

"I'm late, and you're late. I'll meet you back here, babe." He winked at me. I laughed. The wink was so cheesy. Not that I was judging him. I was more amused than anything.

Most girls had a boyfriend, went to prom, and lived happily ever after … until summer, that is. Summer always changed relationships. Summer was on its way. Why were we starting this thing up?

Did everything in my life have to be so complicated?

Chapter 8

The day was all too long. Cindy was missing from lunch. I had to sit with some of my AP English classmates. All they talked about was their parents. They quoted their mothers' every word. Their mom liked this and that. Why did their mom think she could shop at Forever 21? Why did she hate their boyfriend? Whatever, whatever. I had my share of complaints about my trendy mom, but there were far more interesting things to do at lunch than talk about my parents. For one thing, I was bursting at the seams with this "Cameo" secret. And then there was the whole Jason thing. Plus, I wanted to discuss the strategy for 4 p.m. I started to text the whole thing to Cindy after I thought up the name "Project Cameo." I was even writing in spy code: "Your mission, should you choose to accept it, is simple. At 1600 hours you will …" etc., etc., etc.

Fortunately, I remembered that a real spy would never leave a paper trail. The last thing I needed was some trouble getting my cap and gown or a big question mark above my name in the yearbook because Cindy had forwarded the message to a few of her other friends. Sometimes Cindy was a little unpredictable. Plus, Jane had a habit of rifling through Cindy's cell phone during gym class while the teacher took attendance.

It was 2:05 p.m. Jason should've been there to meet me five minutes ago. Conveniently enough, I didn't know his class schedule. But it was less than two months to graduation; it would be silly to try to learn it now. It was better for him to be concerned with my schedule instead.

I had two hours to kill before the mission. Suddenly, these really big, warm hands covered my eyes. "Guess who?"

"I don't know. Is it the guy who was supposed to be here five minutes ago?"

"It is if he is talking to the girl who won't cut him any slack."

I definitely heard Jason. He let his hands down and met me with an unmistakably gorgeous smile.

"My last teacher wanted to go over my term project with me," he said.

My cell phone buzzed.

"What are you doing?" Cindy texted.

"In hall," I texted.

"Meet front entrance 3:45," she texted.

"Inside building," I texted.

"Who u wit," Cindy texted.

"New beau."

"Ew-u, beau so last semester."

"Feeling nostalgic."

Jason rubbed elbows with me.

"What are you doing?"

"I don't know. Do you want to get something to eat?" he asked.

"You have practice today."

"Word. At three," he said.

"Let's get smoothies," I said.

www.CameoTheNovel.com

"You seem like more of a frappuccino girl to me," he said.

"Ah, you have a lot to learn," I said. That was my best try at sounding mysterious.

"Can we meet earlier, will be free at 3," I texted Cindy.

"Who are you texting?" Jason asked.

"Were you looking over my shoulder? You know I have privacy issues as it is," I said. I put my hand on his broad chest and pushed him away from me. "It was just Cindy," I said. "Babe," I added. Then I laughed. It was all so odd.

"You know, I like it when you call me that," he said.

Was that a joke? I hated it when guys said things like they were jokes but really meant them. It was their sly way of seeing your reaction to how they really felt.

Although we'd just shared our likes and dislikes and hobbies and all that getting-to-know-you stuff at the pizza joint/smoothie palace around the corner, I wasn't ready to kiss him yet. I'm sure Cindy knew far less about Peter before she had gotten entangled with him, yet I was kind of prudish, I guess. I hate that word—prude—it reminded me of a prune, all dried up and wrinkly.

I was about to be bum-rushed by every student celebrating the final school bell of the day in two minutes. Jason and I stood silently in the quiet hallway.

"Well, thanks for lunch."

"Lunch?" Apparently that was the wrong term in his book.

"A snack," I corrected myself.

"So can I pick you up tomorrow?" he asked.

I waited five seconds before I answered to add to my mysterious demeanor. "I guess that could work," I said.

www.UndercoverStarlet.com

"Guess?"

"That's right. I guess. Babe," I said.

"Nia!" Cindy yelled from the other end of the hallway as she spearheaded the student body walking behind her toward the exit. Oh gosh, I watched his every move as he came closer to me, pretending I didn't hear Cindy calling me. I found myself leaning back away from him. He came very close to my face. I put my hand on his cheek. I closed my eyes and held my breath. He kissed my cheek.

"Relax," he said.

I was disappointed. The heck with that stupid note, I wanted to spend the whole afternoon with him. But this was yet another way to burn out a relationship, spending too much time with your boyfriend. I watched Cindy gallop down the hallway after she'd gotten an eyeful of Jason and me. Jason looked at his watch. Cindy waited for me at our locker.

"I'm going to walk you to your locker."

"Okay," I said.

He put his arm around me while the crowds of kids passed us. I guessed anybody who didn't know before would know now.

"This is official. Right?"

Was he asking me or telling me? "If you're asking, then, yeah, we're official," I said.

"Are you hanging around school?"

"No."

"Oh."

"Why?"

"I could've given you a ride home."

Had I just lied to my boyfriend? That must be a record—they were going out for sixty seconds before she lied to him. Ever notice that when you tell a small lie, it feels like you've left your body just for the part of the conversation that was the lie and returned just in time for the truth? It's like when I said "no," I didn't really say "no." I wouldn't lie to my boyfriend.

"Well, I might be around for a few minutes, you know, but ... uh ... I won't be here that late. I'll get a ride with Cindy," I said.

"So I'll call you tomorrow to pick you up."

"Yes. Bye." I smiled.

I turned to Cindy who was soaking up every moment of this. I couldn't shake the smile off my face.

"In case you didn't realize it, you are now part of the after-school report," Cindy said.

"What after-school report?" I asked.

"We just started it last week for seniors only. It's the 411 on everything prom. According to this, you may be back in the running for prom queen. An anonymous person is encouraging people to submit you for the write-in vote," Cindy said.

I jerked her arm to see what she was talking about. "This is unreal." I took her phone out of her hand, hit reply, and started to type: "Nia is not going to prom. She's boycotting it. Do not vote for her. Rumors about her new boyfriend aren't true." I pressed send.

"What did you just do?" Cindy was in utter disbelief.

"I'm ensuring that I will not be thrown back onto the popularity bandwagon for one last ride. Having a popular boyfriend suddenly makes me eligible again to be prom queen. It's absurd!"

"I can't believe you did that from my phone," Cindy said.

"How am I supposed to know that you didn't want me to do that? You were the one dangling your cell phone with the afternoon report on it in front of me. You owe me this. I let you in on the popular secret society stuff."

Cindy got quiet. She looked down the hallway. The multitude of kids had thinned down to a handful of individuals casually strolling along.

Cindy pulled me to the side. She looked behind her. Then she looked both ways down the hall. She waited for some underclassmen to pass us by before she uttered a word. "You didn't tell anyone about this, did you?" she whispered.

"No. Did you?" I asked.

"Of course not. Now, I may dibble and dabble in the gossip mill, but I don't want to be dragged underneath it. There are certain lines you just don't cross," Cindy said.

Dibble and dabble. Yeah, right. Who was she kidding? She was the Gossip Mafia. The text I had sent from her phone would be in the morning text probably at the top of the page as an answer to this new after-school report.

"Forget this prom queen nonsense. Let's get a move on. Where were you at lunch today?" I led the way to the point of the mission: namely, the basement.

"With Peter."

"Really, are you guys …?" I asked.

"Yup, pretty much like you and Jason. At least until prom anyway. I'm an independent girl. Who knows whom the summer will bring," Cindy said.

www.CameoTheNovel.com

"Yesterday I wouldn't even admit I liked Jason, and today I'm calling him babe," I said. I was even smitten that he liked it.

"Like you never thought you two would end up together," Cindy said.

"I just got wind of this popular society thing like yesterday. I've been thinking about it. It's like if you're not inducted into it in freshman year, you're left in social limbo for the rest of your years here! Unless you date a popular guy. That's the only loophole. It's completely ridiculous," I said.

"Is it? I mean I don't mind going to all the hot parties and dating the guys with the best cars," Cindy said.

I had realized that there were many issues on which Cindy and I wouldn't see eye to eye. I found myself with nothing more to say. There was no further delaying the upcoming task. I checked my cell phone for the time. It would take us nearly half an hour to navigate through the dark, dingy basement quietly in heels. You could barely see anything with the cheap fluorescent lights they put down there.

"We should've put on our gym sneakers."

"I don't think so. What if someone saw me looking like one of those athletic girls?" Cindy said.

We went quietly down the back staircase—the staircase behind the main staircase. No one ever used it. Good thing, because if anyone spotted us in the basement they would definitely wonder what we were doing there. No one went to the basement without a reason, which led me to wonder: Whoever these secret society people were, how were they getting to the basement?

"Do you think they take the elevator down here?" I whispered to Cindy.

It was weird. The basement was like two flights down from the main floor—kind of scary, actually. Why was it so far underground like a bomb shelter? Probably another reason why it was so undesirable to go down there.

"Why are you saying 'they'? That note referred to one person, as I remember," Cindy said.

"A society implies more than one member," I said sarcastically.

I was starting to think I had brought the wrong person along for the job. "Did you ask anyone if they knew anything about this?" I asked.

"No," Cindy sighed, disappointed. "Why?" she continued.

"Well, we need to know where to look. The note was vague. Is it on the east side of the building or the west side? We can't just go walking through the center of the basement, because if someone comes, we'll be in plain sight," I said.

"True. But what if the person coming is one of them?" Cindy said.

"Precisely! I knew I brought you along for a reason," I said.

"Whatever. I don't know the deal on this society, but I have heard of two girls being blacked out from the yearbook in the past three years," Cindy said.

"Well, they sought me out. I'm not trying to blow the whistle." I couldn't believe I had just stolen a cliché from Taekwon-do Girl.

"Could you say it any louder?" Cindy said.

"It's one of the members who's following me and doing scary stuff," I whispered.

"Like what?"

www.CameoTheNovel.com

Cameo by Tanille

"That sticky Kool-Aid in the bathroom. 'Cameo' in red lipstick on the wall across from my bio class. Do you need more?"

"So you think this is connected to the person you saw in your house?"

"Of course!"

We slowly crept through the stairwell. Cindy pointed to the door. We hid behind the stairwell door. Cindy pushed me in front of her. If there was a sacrifice to be made, it was clear who was going first.

"What if we stay in the stairwell and follow someone to the meeting? I mean, freshmen are so clueless, they wouldn't think to look back behind them to see if we were following them," I said.

"You're so right," Cindy said.

My cell phone started to ring. I quickly whipped it out of my pocket and flipped through the modes to turn it on silent. Why were there five modes to go through before you reached silent? Shouldn't they prioritize that list by most commonly used? By the time I did activate the silent mode, my phone had stopped ringing.

"Hear that?" Cindy texted.

Plunk, plunk, plunk went the sounds of someone's big feet as made when they hit steps. Someone was on their way to the basement.

"Is that one?" I texted.

"Wait and see," she responded.

It was all so covert and operative-like, ducking down near the staircase door so no one could see us and then having to constantly check my cell phone for messages.

www.UndercoverStarlet.com

"Society," she texted.

"No," I texted. This kid was such an oddball. He had red, wiry hair, braces, chapped lips, a hunched back, and he was like seven feet tall.

"I think so. He's on a team." Cindy was becoming insistent. Most of the popular guys in our class were cute even in freshmen year.

We followed the freshman out of the stairwell and down the hall. The basement was architecturally structured like a hospital. It was made up of four long hallways that created a rectangle with a connecting hallway in the middle. Between that and the pale green on the walls, that place had "institution" written all over it. I couldn't believe this kid didn't suspect anything. If I were a member of a secret society, I would double and triple check to make sure no one saw me doing anything—not even breathing funny, let alone walking to a meeting. This guy hadn't looked over his shoulder once. Good for us. We were able to covertly follow him down the hall. Walking quietly in heels was an art.

I once watched a movie about secret societies, starring these two insanely hot actors. It's kind of like how girls buy an album just for the pictures. The content is meaningless at this age. Anyway, they killed this guy for sneaking into a meeting. I guess being blacked out of the yearbook ranked right up there with death to some. Imagine not appearing on record as having attended high school. Now add to that the fear of getting into an altercation at any time whenever you used the bathroom at school, at home, or at someone else's house. The mere thought was vexing me. What was with the bathroom? Was it because I was alone in the bathroom, like when I was alone in my room? If I could figure out a connection, maybe I could stop this.

www.CameoTheNovel.com

I spotted a janitor's closet.

"Try opening the closet door. I'll keep an eye on the suspect," I texted.

"It opened!" she texted.

I was surprised yet relieved. We finally had some cover. Cindy and I hid behind the janitor's closet door while watching the redhead continue down the hall. I mean, we couldn't very well follow him up to the meeting door. But the cover did not come without consequences. It smelled like a wet, dirty mop laced with bleach in there. It was hard to concentrate. All I could think about was that nasty mop.

"I think I got an idea," Cindy texted.

She dug her hand into her tiny little handbag, and a giant compact emerged. She flipped open the compact.

"Get in the closet," she whispered.

Were we talking now? "I don't want to get locked in here."

"Just trust me." She cracked the door and slid the mirror portion of the compact out the crack. Then Cindy flipped the mirror in the opposite direction. I tried my best not to touch anything in that germ-infested place. Who knows what ringworm and wart germs were in there? Touch one thing in there, next thing you know some microbe will be growing on your skin. I shivered at the thought.

"Oh, snap," Cindy said as she let the door slam.

"Why did you let the door slam?" No real spy slams doors.

"Sorry."

I used my cell phone as a light. The fear of bumping into something dirty was haunting me.

"It's Jason."

"Who?" I asked.

"He's coming down the hall," she said.

"Do they have basketball down here?" I asked.

"No," Cindy said.

"Where did the freshman go?"

"Wait, there's more. Carolina is right behind him."

"Are they together?"

"I don't know."

"And now that you slammed the door, a mirror hanging out of the janitor's closet will look suspicious," I complained.

"Just give me a second." Cindy cracked the door once more as quietly as she could. This time she peeked out to see if they had passed the closet. Then she slowly slipped the mirror out of the crack at the bottom of the door.

"Good thinking. No one will look down there," I said.

"Okay, she's too skinny to be Carolina. She's like a stick. Oh! Guess what!"

"Just tell me."

"They're going into the weight room."

"The sweaty weight room?"

"It's Lucy!"

This was worse than I thought. "I know Jason is not interested in her," I said.

"Like he would be interested in Carolina," Cindy said.

"No, but I think she's part of the whole thing. And if they were together, that would mean he's part of it too."

We were both silent. What was the next move?

"There's only one thing to do," Cindy said.

"The weight room," we both said.

Cindy cringed in disgust. I didn't mind encountering foul B.O. to get to the bottom of this. It was the airborne bacteria that had me spooked. We cracked the door open.

"Okay, no one is coming up the hallway," Cindy said.

She stuck her compact out of the door crack with the mirror facing the opposite direction so she could see what was going on down at the other end of the hall.

"Clear," she continued.

I stepped out into the hallway first. It was practically impossible to walk quietly in heels when your feet hurt. And there were two pairs of throbbing feet walking to the weight room. Real inconspicuous—Cindy's typical modus operandi. We got to the weight room door, and it was wide open. I didn't hear anything but the AM sports radio playing. That would surely throw any reasonable teenager off the trail. But we weren't reasonable. Rather than peeking in and pussyfooting around, I stormed right inside. I was surrounded by sweaty weight machines and dumbbells.

Cindy tapped me on the shoulder. "Where is everyone?" she asked.

I shrugged.

"... the secret passageway?"

"You know, Michelle is exactly who I want to be like," a coy, female voice with a British accent said from the hallway.

"Is that right?' Craig said.

"It figures! Craig is a member," I said.

www.UndercoverStarlet.com

Cindy rolled her eyes. "Hence your stint on the popularity scene," she said.

"Don't remind me," I said.

"You know she commands everything." The girl's voice was getting closer.

"They're coming in here," I said.

"Duh, Sherlock," Cindy said.

It was between the closet and the coach's office. How would we explain barging into the coach's office?

"Oh my god, I am not going into some pitch-black room. What if we get locked in?" Cindy asked.

"Now you're above hiding in a closet. You did it like three minutes ago," I said. I went inside the Dungeons & Dragons–looking utility closet.

"Where the heck is the light switch?" Cindy asked.

"You cannot stand there with the door open."

I took my cell phone out to use it as a light. There was like one of those overhead basement bulbs in the middle of the room with a pull chain.

"Did this room invent the word 'antiquated' or what?" Cindy was growing impatient with the mission I could see.

I stood at the door with one eye peeking into the weight room, hoping to get a glance of Craig and Michelle's adoring fan. No such luck! They were gone. How could people keep disappearing in the basement like that? After quietly closing the door, I had a chance to look at the room. It really was a supply closet. There was no secret door or anything. Like anybody popular with a shred of dignity would walk through this eyesore to get to their society cave. Even though I had discovered a few gems hiding in there.

"Check out these brand-new elliptical machines. Just as we're graduating, they decide to upgrade the gym with something electronic!" I said.

"It's about time!" Cindy said.

"Shhh! Wait. It sounds like someone is walking," I said.

"Go see," Cindy said.

"No, what if they're coming in here? Turn the light off."

It took me a few seconds to muster up the courage to see who was at the door. I just didn't want to open it and have someone staring at me on the other side. I cracked the door. Phew. There was no one standing there. I stole a quick glance through a crack in the door without being noticed.

"Jason," I whispered. He was back into this whole mess.

"Is he alone?" Cindy asked.

"Yeah, he's going into the coach's office." Was it actually possible that the coach was in on this?

"Don't freak out. He is so in the bag," Cindy said.

"Last time I used the words 'in the bag,' I got a B minus on my bio exam," I said.

The question was who *wasn't* in on this? Now might have been a good time to disclose that I had no idea who the Coach was or what team he coached for. The only words on the door read coach. He didn't even have to be a real coach. How deep of a secret was this society? The coach's office could've been the real meeting place, and maybe there was no coach at all.

"I'm going over there," I said.

www.UndercoverStarlet.com

Cindy grabbed my arm firmly, like a parent harnessing a stubborn, spoiled child. "You do like him, don't you?" she asked.

I was silent.

"You're getting out of hand. I'm counting on six people for our limo. Unless you want to kick in for two seats, I wouldn't go over there," Cindy said.

Every once in a while she surprised me. This wasn't about the prom limo. I knew that she knew that I really dug him. Too bad! I couldn't let my feelings for a boy run my life.

"We should go. I mean there is only so long I can stay in this eight-by-four closet," I said.

"I know, I get claustrophobic in my ten-by-ten walk-in closet at home," Cindy said.

I opened the door. It couldn't have been any noisier. The loud, creaking sound alluded to the need of some WD40 on the hinges. If there was a cat to be let out of the bag, it was definitely on its way out. The door marked Coach was closed.

"All clear," I whispered to Cindy. I stepped into the middle of the gym. "Ouch. Could you not step on the back of my shoe?" I said.

"Actually, those are my shoes anyway," Cindy said.

Right then, I noticed that there was something underneath the leg press. "Do you see that?" I mean, this could've been some mirrored illusion.

"That white hat? Absolutely." Cindy snatched that hat up with contempt. Her eyes scoured every inch of that hat, inside and out. She turned up one long blonde hair and one short brown hair.

Suddenly, Jason opened the door. He was standing at the doorway with the door cracked and his attention was focused on someone sitting behind the desk. I couldn't really see them. Cindy and I made like two Corvettes and left in him our dust. FYI: That's going to be the first car that I buy myself. A Corvette.

Chapter 9

We were almost at my house. Riding in Cindy's car was fabulous! It was a beauty, a shiny black Thunderbird convertible with super-soft cream leather seats. She almost always had the top down. I loved it when the breeze blew through my hair. For a few moments, I felt optimistic, like life was for the taking.

"Your mom was so glad your father decided to get his car fixed," I said.

"That was no coincidence. If you want things to happen, you have to make them happen. Much like how I merely reminded my mother that our life seemed to be shrinking right before our eyes. My dad downscaled the new kitchen remodel! Then he attempted to slash the backyard landscaping budget in half, eliminating the fire pit and grill. I mean, it was really up to her to save us from ridicule. I only insinuated that my uncle may have been right. We were becoming a discount family. On her side of the family, we're the only ones who drive American cars."

Cindy's Thunderbird coupe, which cost more than most of the teachers' cars at our school, was apparently the equivalent of bumming around. She did have a knack for getting her way, though.

"Nice work. Resurfacing insecurities in the heart of your mother can be an effective way to get things done," I said.

"Don't judge me. You would turn on anyone in a heartbeat if they represented popularity or narcissism. In my book, that makes you as shallow—just with bigger words," Cindy said.

"That is so not true. I never turn on people."

"What about Alyssa and Cassie?"

"What about them?"

"The second you stopped getting the gossip text, all of a sudden you weren't friends. You were boycotting the popular people when you made it seem like it was them who didn't want to be friends with you. They really liked you."

"They're Jane's friends, not mine. The two of them combined couldn't fill out one college application. They had to have 'assistance' for that. What do we have in common?"

"So you're smart! You're an intellectual snob."

"I am not a snob." I couldn't believe she had just called me that! It hurt most because Cindy knew me best. I let out a heavy sigh. I had to just shake that off.

Cindy and I drove the rest of the way to my house in silence. The tree-lined streets were quiet. She pulled up to my house. I was a little scared. I clutched the door handle tightly.

"Are you coming?" I didn't want to go in alone.

My street just didn't look the same. All I could see were places where someone could hide—an overgrown bush in someone's yard, a tree with a thick trunk over in front of the neighbor's house. I could've had an anxiety attack right then and there.

"No, I'm not coming. I don't feel appreciated."

Are you kidding me? "Trust me. I couldn't have walked here from your house. I definitely appreciate the ride."

"I'll wait out here. I have to make some calls."

"Fine."

I opened the door. It felt kind of weird. Like I should have taken a look around outside before I walked inside. There was no one around on the block. Cindy sat in her car, quietly edging toward carpal tunnel syndrome with her super-speed texting. The alarm went off. After racing against the nano-second clock to plug in the code, I strolled upstairs to pick up some more of my own clothes and shoes. God, I needed to wear my own flats! The balls of my feet were burning! I didn't take those shoes off all day for fear that I wouldn't be able to get them back on my pulsating feet. One day in Cindy's shoes and I'd told off my ex, snagged a new man, played secret agent, and been stalked. Too much excitement for this intellectual snob.

The doorbell rang. My heart skipped a beat. Was this trouble? I mean, Cindy would call me if something strange went down outside, right? If she noticed! I was ultra-paranoid at this point. Maybe it was just a friendly neighbor. I tried to clear my mind as I strolled down the steps. The doorbell rang again. I looked out the window. Cindy was standing at the door with Jason. Before I could open the door all the way, Cindy pushed the door open. She looked at her watch.

"I'm expecting a phone call." She raised her eyebrows and looked at me funny as if I was supposed to know what that meant. Maybe she was waiting for Peter to call.

"He is not seeing Lucy," she continued.

"That was discreet." I couldn't believe she had asked him.

"He says he doesn't know her, and I believe him."

I turned Cindy around and pushed her in the direction of her car. "Do you want to come in?" I asked Jason. "Completely embarrassed" would've summed up how I felt. Before I could close the door behind him, Cindy had wedged her foot in it.

www.CameoTheNovel.com

"Cindy?" I said. She motioned her finger for me to come closer.

"Before you two set it off, just know I have to leave in like fifteen minutes. We have to stop by the coffee house in the mall to meet Roger."

"We?"

"One who needs a ride accompanies one who has a car."

"Are you coming in or ...?" She moved her foot. "So what are you doing here?" I asked.

"Hi," he said.

"Hi. Would you like something to drink?"

"I thought you were going to question me first."

I could've melted at the sound of his voice, but first things first. "I heard that you and Lucy were seen together in the basement after school when you said that ..." I had to stop. I had caught myself playing the insecure jealous girlfriend role. I guess I should've been that girl when I was dating Craig. There I was, one relationship too late.

Could I tell him that I thought someone was stalking me without sounding self-centered? I mean why would someone be after me?

"It's just been strange lately," I said.

"Like the lipstick on the wall?"

"Yeah. Lucy might have something to do with it," I said.

"And?" he said.

"Do you know her?" I asked.

"Are you asking me or accusing me? Because you sound

like you're accusing," he said.

"Ha! I keep trying, believe me," I said. He looked more than annoyed—"perturbed" would be a great adjective to describe the contempt in his eyes. I didn't care. So the novelty of our love/hate thing was wearing off. Good. Now I could see the real him. Maybe he only thought he liked me. You know, those guys who like you until they find out you have something going on upstairs, otherwise known as brain function. Then, all of a sudden, they're interested in some flunky cheerleader, more interested in her eye shadow color than taking an AP test for college credit. Who needed a future when purple was the new it color for the season?

One might wonder why I couldn't just let go and let him like me and care about me in the melodramatic way every normal teenage girl dreamed of. I didn't know why I was like this, I just was. Letting go would be like driving a car with your hands off the steering wheel—you're just asking for it.

"I didn't come here for this. I hate the way you play around. You won!" he said.

"Why don't you just answer the question?"

"I don't even know her. I was walking down the steps, and next thing I know she was standing right next to me. I went to the basement to meet with my training coach. This girl who gave you a report, uh, they tell you that? Did they say I talked to her? That would mean I know her."

"I saw you. I'm sorry I didn't say it at first. I just want to figure this out. I do trust you." I stopped for a moment. Was I telling a white lie? Or did I just say the T word? I wanted to trust him. "Want" and "do" should be synonyms. I guess there are a lot of things that should be. I looked at him, and I knew what I had to do.

www.CameoTheNovel.com

"At the party yesterday, someone accosted me in the bathroom and insisted that the first bathroom incident was part of this secret society prank. I don't know who's doing it or why this is happening. I got a note in homeroom today about this meeting in the basement. I assumed the person behind these pranks, including the lipstick thing, would be there. But we couldn't find the meeting."

Jason was quiet for a moment. "If you got that note in homeroom, why didn't you say anything?"

"I don't know. It's supposed to be secret."

"All right."

What if he was a member and this was part of their front? "So how did you become popular?" I asked.

"I transferred here sophomore year. I joined the basketball team, and I made friends. Then people from the team introduced me to other people—how people usually make friends," he said.

"So you're not a member of the secret society?" I asked.

"I don't really know what it is," he said.

I felt a ten-pound weight lift off my back. I was relieved. It was hard to accuse him. My eyes gazed at his lips expectantly. Now would be a good time to make a move, lover boy.

"Cindy," he blurted out.

"What?" I asked.

"She's in the window," he said.

I went and opened the door. I flashed Cindy a fake smile. "Hi. Welcome to Casa Nia. How can I help you?"

"I need a cup of water. I had two cappuccinos at lunch. I'm

www.UndercoverStarlet.com

totally parched," Cindy said.

I held the door open. "I take it you've gotten your call?" I asked.

"They always call."

Jason waited for Cindy to leave the room. "Forget these urban legends."

"I feel like at any moment I could be kidnapped or attacked. It has me all freaked out. I have to do something about it."

"Did you hear that?" he said.

"A scream?"

I hurried to the kitchen, and Jason followed. Cindy was still screaming. It sounded as if she had been strangled by the neck. It was a life-or-death type of thing. The screams got louder as we got closer.

It was a quick sprint from the front foyer to the kitchen. The refrigerator door was open.

"Oh, my God!" Cindy shrieked.

"Yo, the back door," Jason said.

The back door was wide open, and the porch light was on.

"Hello?" Jason moved with apprehension as he slowly stepped outside. I went to the door and watched him. I looked left, then right. Not a single leaf stirred. Whoever was here was long gone. They could've been hiding, though. There was no time to think about that.

"Cindy?" I called out.

"Nia!" she screamed.

"I think she's inside."

It was so hard to tell where the screams were coming from. Jason jumped inside the house. I made sure to lock the door behind him. Whoever had been here had to have left from that door because we always kept it locked.

Jason looked in the bathroom and under the stairs. "Nothing," he said.

"Check the basement," I said.

"This door here?"

"Yeah." I was right behind Jason.

"Nia! Where have you been?" Cindy sounded like she was on the brink of tears. I hesitated to turn on the light. I couldn't believe this was all because of me. Whatever had happened to Cindy somehow had something to do with my loose ends. I felt so wretched.

"Is there a light?" Jason asked as he reached the bottom of the stairs.

A sliver of light crept through the dusty basement window. Dusk was approaching. I was apprehensive going down the stairs. I had never seen Cindy like this.

Cindy had been thrown three or four feet from the stairs. "What happened?"

"I can't get up," Cindy said dryly.

I turned on the light. Cindy was lying right at the bottom of the stairs. Before I could stop myself, I let out a huge gasp. I tried to pretend it hadn't happened. If Cindy thought that cut was half as bad as I thought it was, she was going to go into all-out panic mode. She had a gaping gash in her leg. It was pretty bloody. It wasn't terribly large, but it was a hole, for sure. Her hair was a mess, like she'd rolled down a hill. Her makeup was smudged underneath her eyes. I could tell some tears had run down her face.

"Is your leg all right?" Jason asked her.

"Yeah, I just have problems with my knee sometimes because of an ice skating injury when I was eleven," Cindy said.

I was slow to make my way down the stairs. Jason picked Cindy up and carried her to the couch where he put her down. "Who did this?" he asked.

Cindy was slow to answer.

"Do you have a concussion?" I asked.

"No," she said.

I dialed the police on my cell phone. The line was busy. How could 911 be busy in the middle of the day?! Things had gone from bad to horrific! I redialed the police.

"Tell me what happened," I said.

"I was in the refrigerator, and someone put a hand over my mouth. They had on a smelly cheap black glove. It smelled like pleather. They grabbed me from behind. I tried to take their hand off my mouth. They had my other hand behind my back. I could barely move. Then they threw me down the stairs. Did you see the scrape on my leg?" I shook my head, no. Cindy glanced at it. "I hope it doesn't scar."

The police picked up. What was with 911 around here? "Someone just broke into my house. I live at Eighty-Nine Chester Street. It was a break-in. They assaulted my friend. They threw her down the stairs. ... I don't know. They might've entered through the basement. ... Yes, there is a back door. It was open too. But it was locked. ... Don't break down the front door. We're going to move upstairs. ... Yeah, I think she can move. ... I don't know. I don't think it is broken. Okay." I hung the phone up. "They're going to send a medic," I said.

"He said something to me. He sounded kind of gay, though. Like, manly, but he talked like a valley girl," she said.

"What did he say?" I asked.

"I think I hear some cars upstairs, babe."

Jason was like my bionic guy with his supersonic hearing. He ran his hand across my back, and I flinched a little. It'd been so long since a guy had touched me like that. I put his hand on my waist.

"Excuse me, I'm hurt here. If they're upstairs, shouldn't we go?"

Needless to say, Cindy knew how to command a room.

"I'll take her upstairs." Jason picked Cindy up and carried her upstairs. I walked behind him pulling on the back of his shirt. He was so good to me and my friends. Who said chivalry was dead? Oh, yeah, every pop song on the radio maybe.

"He said to tell you that you're next," Cindy blurted out somewhere between the dining room and the front hallway. Jason put her down on the couch.

"Why are they after me?" I asked Jason. Why didn't people make trouble for the creeps like Michelle? "It could've been a girl. Did he have a white hat on?" I asked.

Jason peeked through the curtains.

"No. I didn't get a clear look at him. No. No. I do know he had on a black mask or a ski mask or something. But it was black."

"Are they here?" I asked Jason.

"No." He looked out the window again.

www.UndercoverStarlet.com

"What time is it?" Cindy asked.

"Six-fifty-five," Jason said.

"These things are always somebody you know. Who do you think is running the secret society?" I asked. The police were banging on the door.

"I'll get it," Jason said.

Well, it was official. I was in big trouble. They were going to contact my parents and the whole nine. I was sure of it. I wondered if these things happened to members of the secret society. What if somehow these popular kids had power outside of school? Okay, that was completely ridiculous. Obviously I'd seen one too many movies.

I was going to let Cindy and Jason speak with the uniforms first, in an effort to prolong making this report official. I was a little scared. What if this could ruin my life? I didn't know what I had gotten into. Either these people stalking me were punks or they were real. Suffice it to say I would have trouble sleeping tonight.

Jason held the door open. The lead detective walked inside. Two other uniforms followed behind him. I have to say he was kind of hot, in the distant I'm-not-dead-yet sort of way. He was black with jet-black hair in a crew cut, nice, brown skin, and almond-shaped eyes. He was built but lean.

"Detective Smart," he said. The detective shook Jason's hand. "Who called the police? Was it you?" he asked Jason.

"No," Jason said.

"I did," I said.

"Is this your house, miss?" he asked

"Yes, someone broke in. I think through the basement window or something because all the doors were locked. Then they attacked my friend. Cindy, tell them how you were at the refrigerator and someone attacked you," I said.

"I was looking for something in fridge, and then somebody grabbed me with a grimy black glove …" Cindy said.

"And tell them how he said I was next," I said.

"I will, if you take a breath and let me talk," Cindy said.

After reliving the same story from varying angles, we got to the meat and potatoes of everything. "Do you kids have any guess as to who this could be?" Detective Smart asked.

"Already been there. Try Roger McEvans to start," Cindy said.

"Smart, come look at this," the rookie said.

"One sec." Detective Smart wanted to finish his notes. "Who else do you think might have done this?" Detective Smart looked at Cindy.

She shrugged.

"Michelle," I said.

Cindy grabbed me by the collar. "I just want you to know you just blacklisted all of us. Let me break it down. 'All of us' includes Mr. Knight-in-Shining-Armor over there. Think about that," she whispered under her breath.

"Didn't you say it was a guy?" Detective Smart said.

"Yes, I did." Cindy sounded all too gleeful.

"We don't know if Michelle did it herself but she could've sent someone. That's conspiracy at a minimum … right?" I said.

Cindy rolled her eyes. "Just perfect, Ms. Know-It-All!" she said

www.UndercoverStarlet.com

under her breath.

"Do you have her last name?" the detective asked.

"No," Cindy said.

"Does she go to your school?"

"No," Cindy blurted out.

"Yes," I said.

Everyone became quiet.

"Look, we don't think that she did this, but I think she may know who did this," I said.

"Why?" he asked.

"I don't know. She hates me," I said.

"I'm imagining that there could be other kids at school that hate you too?" he said.

"No, I think you may be imagining wrong," Jason said angrily.

I can't believe I had thought the detective was cute.

"I know where you can find Roger right now," Cindy said.

"Where?" he asked.

"At the coffee house in the mall on Old Creek Manor."

"Wait!" I yelled.

Everyone in the room slowly turned to me. I guess it sounded as if I'd had a revelation. "My gut tells me that Roger is innocent," I said.

Detective Smart rolled his eyes. The rookie detective in the back laughed under his breath. I turned my back to the detectives and whispered to Jason. "Did I just sound like a super sleuth or something?"

"It's cool," Jason said. Was he always this calm?

"Back to Roger, think about it. Roger barely weighs 130 pounds, who the heck could he overpower? Second, he's head over heels for Cindy. He would never push her down the stairs. And I've never talked to him before this week. I don't think he hates me," I said.

"He doesn't," Jason said.

Detective Smart was taking all of this down in his tiny pad.

"We need to head back to Cindy's house. My mother is out of town on business until tomorrow, and I'm staying at Cindy's house. How much longer will this take?" I said.

"This is a crime scene. Sorry. I can't take pictures with my mobile and send you a text message with an update later on. Someone has to take a look at your friend's busted leg. They have to process the doors for fingerprints and the floor for footprints," he said.

"Awesome! The county has a forensics budget for break-ins. Maybe they can pick up the tab for my broken heel. These shoes were $130," Cindy said.

Jason was looking kind of worried.

"I have to get some things from upstairs. That's why we stopped by here, so I could pick up some of my stuff," I said.

"Okay. But don't be long."

I shook my head. "Um, it might be safer if Jason escorted me upstairs."

"Miss, we've already secured the house, but he can go with you. Be back soon," Detective Smart mumbled under his breath while taking notes.

"Cindy, you should make sure nothing was stolen out of your car," I added.

Cindy was practically frantic. She hopped up and limped out the door.

"Wait, wait!" the detective yelled after her. That should keep him busy for a while. He pulled out his walkie-talkie. "Still waiting for backup at Eighty-Nine Chester Street. Over," he said.

Jason and I walked up the stairs. He walked in front of me. I grabbed his hand, and he glanced over his shoulder. I was in so much fear I started biting my nails, something I never do. In my head, we had already gone out, broken up, made up, and gone out again. I couldn't shake the feeling I had built up over the past forty-some odd days that it was inevitable for a guy to cheat.

Just let go! That's what I kept saying in my head. Maybe my fear of breaking up was the problem.

"Down the hall on the right," I said.

Well, he was about to enter my bedroom. Jason stopped in front of the door and waited for me to go inside.

"Well, you know what we have to do," I whispered to him.

"What?" He asked eagerly.

"Close the door, slowly," I said. Once I was sure the door was closed, I resumed my normal tone. "We have to find Michelle and get to the bottom of this."

He didn't say anything, but the way he shook his head matched my sentiment exactly. If Michelle was behind all of this somehow, she was definitely crazier than we thought.

"I just can't take this anymore! We have to do something, something big. I mean what if … I'm not sure. What if this is only the beginning?" I said.

"I think the forensic scientists downstairs got this on lock. Somebody should be put away or on charges by tomorrow."

Okay. So I knew this was the worst time to be thinking it, but if this continued for another day or two, when would be a good time to kiss him? Would it be like fire, you know, like this explosion of passion? Or would it be sweet enough to steal my breath away? Or would it be like kissing your brother—just downright vile? Uh, please, it could not be the last one! He was definitely too fly. Plus, I didn't even have a brother.

I didn't want to do anything but kiss him. To feel him so close to me was everything I had wanted. It was what having a boyfriend meant to me, I guess. For a moment it seemed like time everywhere had stopped, and all we had to do was kiss. He caught me staring at him. *Yikes! There goes my cover.* I was supposed to play it cool. Jeez, the pressures of living all in my head were too much sometimes.

I packed a few outfit options for the next day and snagged a pair of shoes. "Can you carry my bag downstairs?"

"I got it."

"I shouldn't have accused you earlier," I said. I wanted to get back to our good place. Maybe I should tell him that. Then again, post-Craig, I have a policy against baring all the first week of dating.

"No issue. It wasn't a thing. I didn't know this was so serious. This whole stalking society … thing," he said.

I looked out the window, searching for something to remind me that tomorrow would come, and lo and behold, I set my eyes upon that white hat! Across the street in the neighbors' yard was a girl in a white pageboy cap. Either this was the

www.UndercoverStarlet.com

must-have accessory of the summer or this was the work of the infamous secret society. Why didn't I just call a spade a spade?

"Babe, come here!" I called.

Jason smiled. Was he thinking what I had been thinking five minutes before? I counted in my head as he walked to me with lust in his eyes. *One Mississippi, two Mississippi, three Mississippi.* He stood as close as he could to me without touching me. He leaned into me slowly. Too bad, it was back to reality! No kissing, yet!

I turned my head to the window. "See that girl across the street?" I asked.

"With that white hat on?" He said it like the white hat was a dangerous, contagious virus or something.

"Guess I shouldn't wear a white hat tomorrow, huh?" I said.

"Nah, you could wear anything and it'd look good," he said.

"Babe, we have to go get that girl."

"Why? What do you mean 'get'?"

"We need to question her!"

"Who is she?"

"I don't know. She's part of that idiot society."

"How do you know?"

"The infamous white hat!" I shouted.

"Shhh!" He laughed.

It was the first time he'd laughed all day. I had almost forgotten how cute his laugh was. I hate that infatuation amnesia where your memory is temporarily paralyzed when you fall head over heels for a dude. You forget what he looks like, what his voice sounds like. But you can't forget his kiss. Ask any ninety-year-old woman about her best kiss and, although she may not remember where she had put her teeth, she'll remember his first and last name, be sure of that.

"Nia, she's gone."

"What?"

"She left."

"Downstairs, now."

We booked out the door. How were we going to get out of the house? Jason froze at the bottom of the stairs. Detective Smart and his mini-me were in the living room.

"Nia, can you look at this?" Detective Smart yelled.

I hurried into the living room. I prayed nothing was missing. That was the last thing I needed. I'd never hear the end of it. Suddenly my cell phone beeped, but the sound of my cell quickly became the second priority upon laying my eyes on the huge grape jelly stain on my mother's white area rug. My mother considered our house her interior designer debut. She dreamed of making interior design her second career. This was definitely going to be an issue. As my eyes drifted upward, I saw it.

"What do they have against chess?" Jason asked.

"Look at this note!" Detective Smart said.

As I walked closer to the detective, I understood why he was shouting. Some wacko wrote a note in grape jelly all over the chess board: YOU'RE DONE LIKE BURNT TOAST!

"Isn't that clever?" the rookie rent-a-cop said.

I rolled my eyes, and Detective Smart followed suit.

"What does that mean to you?" he asked.

"That they've got it in for me. All this forensics ... it's not rocket science," I said. Suddenly I realized I was starting to sound as tart as Cindy.

"Bag this," Detective Smart instructed Rent-a-Cop.

I took that moment to step into my own tennis shoes. My cell was beeping.

"Asked Jane about the secret society for the popular, says they control all the votes for every dance, school election, and prom. They even have who gets to be valedictorian on lock," Cindy texted. I know she did not just say she told Jane. Within the next five minutes everyone in our class would receive a forward on my secret society stalker.

My cell phone beeped again. "Don't spazz out. I told her she would be blacklisted if she told anyone."

The way Cindy acted you would've thought she was part of it—threatening Jane and all. How would I know if she had been inducted freshman year or not?

"Girl outside with white hat. Catch her. Tied up here," I texted.

"When will I be able to lock the house up? Cindy and I have some ... homework to do," I asked the detective. Which reminded me, why did Jason come over in the first place? The detective was obviously ignoring me.

"Do you have an update on the project?" I nodded in Jason's general direction.

"Oh! Snap! I forgot." He walked over to his backpack and pulled some yellow papers out. "My father got these from the archives at his job. We can use these to compare the recession trademarks," he said.

"Indicators," I corrected him.

"Right! Indicators from the past recessions. We can compare to the current economic conditions," he said.

"Excellent." I was all excited. Why? It was just some homework.

"Okay, miss, you can close the house up for now. We have some evidence to take back to the station. But we'll need access to the house tomorrow. We're also going to need your mother's contact information. We need your parents' numbers too, young man. And Cindy ... that's the young lady outside, right?"

Oh, so I was "Miss," but he knew Cindy's name. Why was I surprised? She had that effect on guys.

"Yes." Jason wrote the info down and passed me the paper. I wrote both my mom's info and Cindy's.

"I'll be on the porch. Let me know when it's ready for lock-up," I said.

Jason followed me to the door but not without raising an eyebrow.

"What?" I asked.

"Hmm," he said.

"What's 'hmm'?" I said.

"I thought you were perfect at English, but you personified the house," he said. Was he a closet nerd?

"I did not. Okay, maybe I did a little. Is this an English final?" I asked.

"Maybe we could study together for it." He held the front door open for me. I took my time walking through, enjoying every moment of it. It seemed like it had been forever since I had been the apple of someone's eye.

"I have a plan," he said.

"What's this?" I asked as my eyes fell upon Cindy conversing with someone who looked like the girl in the white hat behind the neighbor's bushes. I could really only speculate because the bushes covered the girl's face. But I usually trusted my gut feeling. Luckily for her, our neighbor refused to cut the bushes that protruded over onto our property. That didn't change the facts, though. The fact was Cindy was talking to a girl. And I just couldn't believe who that girl looked like. Without a doubt, she favored Lucy!

Cindy hated Lucy just as much as I did. Didn't she? Cindy quickly turned to look over her shoulder. I didn't want her to know that I had seen her—at least, not yet. So I did the only thing left to do. I lay one big kiss on Jason's lips to create a diversion. To be honest, I was afraid what might happen next if she knew I had seen her. It was creepy to constantly be afraid of what was going to happen next.

Jason stopped kissing me first. That is not how it was supposed to go. My rule was always to stop kissing a guy first, at least if you could help it. He just stared at me. Apparently he was surprised. Wasn't this what we'd been trying to accomplish all day?

"I need you to give me a ride," I said.

"Okay ... where?" he asked.

I couldn't tell him that I had no clue. "I actually need to make two stops," I said.

"Just as long as it doesn't get me killed," he said.

"Don't joke like that," I said.

Those scary movies were always joking about the most outlandish thing that could happen next. And then what happened? Usually that very thing they'd joked about!

"Nia, can we go now?" Cindy said coyly.

"Well, you should go ahead. We're going to wait here for them to finish so I can lock up. Then we're going to hang out a little." I winked my eye at Cindy. She looked concerned. I guess her secret plan with Lucy would have to wait an hour or two.

"I have a 10 p.m. curfew. And I need you to cover for me so I can sneak out with Peter."

This was unbelievable. Did she expect me to believe her convenient plan to leave me alone?

"Well, I guess that's going to have to be too bad," I said.

Cindy honestly looked terrified.

"Did Jane tell you who the leader of the group was?" I asked.

Cindy was thinking. "You know, I had to cut the conversation short while they bandaged my leg," Cindy said. How convenient.

"Sure she didn't say Michelle, and you forgot?" I asked.

"Huh? It's simply a rumor," she said. Was she lost all of a sudden? "I don't think it's safe to just leave you," she said. How clever. Was this about me now?

"I'll be right back." I walked away from Cindy and Jason. I wasn't going to let her make me choose between her and Jason after seeing what I had just seen.

"Wait up." Cindy hopped along behind me.

"Cindy, you don't need me as a decoy. Just tell your mom we're going to dinner and go meet up with Peter," I said.

"I know what to tell my own mother!" Cindy said defensively.

"After the detective calls your parents and tells them that you were maliciously attacked, I can see how your curfew might change. My suggestion? Go out and enjoy the night. I mean no one's stalking *you*," I said.

"I was not maliciously saying anything. You are blowing this out of proportion!"

"Yeah, says the girl with the bandaged leg. Text me if anything changes."

Detective Smart and his sidekick were on the front porch talking to Jason. Before I could even form an opinion on that, my cell began to ring. I could tell by the ringtone that it was my mother.

"I'm driving her home," Jason told the detective.

"You take her straight home to her grandmother's house. Here's the address," Detective Smart said. He examined Jason's face carefully, and then he glanced at his watch. "Ordinarily, we would drive her home to ensure a safe arrival. You seem like a good kid. And my wife, she hates it when I'm late for dinner," he said.

I looked at him and wondered if that was my future, a-good-looking, matter-of-fact, slightly witty … well, not witty but definitely not dull-witted husband. I know every young girl wants to grow up and get married. But there was something a little claustrophobic about waking up to the same man for the rest of my life. I was only seventeen, after all. Thoughts like that haunted me from time to time. How life could be so definite. I loved change. I wasn't even definite on what I was going to

www.CameoTheNovel.com

wear tomorrow.

In all that time I was thinking, I'd let my mother's call go to voicemail. Oh, well, she'd call back in three minutes, by which time I hoped to be on our way to our first stop. I found myself wishing—if only this were all over and who, what, where, and why were answered. Was that too much to ask? Apparently, anything you wanted in this life you had to work for.

"You've got a phone call. Are you going to answer it?" Detective Smart asked.

What was that all about? Was he trying to discredit me and throw the case out?

"It's my mother," I said. I flashed the screen at the detective so he could see her name pop up. Before I put it away in my back pocket, I cleared the missed call, only to notice a new ringtone downloading.

"What is this?"

"What happened?" the detective asked.

"Oh, it's just a voicemail," I said.

Maybe Jason loaded our song "Cameo" on my phone. Oh, my goodness! Listen to me, "our song." It was kind of nauseating, yet sweet.

"I'll check this after I lock up," I continued.

"We'll wait here," the detective said.

I turned on the theft alarm, and I had thirty seconds to get out the door. I guess one could see how this would be the perfect time to stand in the middle of the floor and ponder on how I had gotten here.

Two months ago I had stood in this exact spot, leaving Craig and the crew waiting for me while I stood in the middle of the floor foolishly thinking I had finally reached my golden days. Little did I know, my whole fairy-tale existence was being orchestrated by a bunch of C-average, over-privileged, self-absorbed airheads. I couldn't understand why the dumbest people somehow ran the school. Yet if they did not, I guess President Bush would have been an anomaly. It seemed like dumb people were trying to run everything.

That was it! Tonight I was going to settle the score for every smart, good-looking, no-nonsense high school senior who'd ever been toyed with by the "popular."

With about one second left before I set off the lasers, I slid out the door. Jason met me on the porch. Detective Smart was serious about his wife's attitude. He was in the squad car with the engine running. They waved to me on the porch.

"Get home safely. Call down to the station if there are problems. Drive safe, Jason." Detective Smart pulled off. Cindy was still parked in the driveway.

"What's the deal?" I yelled.

"I didn't want to leave until you guys left," she said.

"Do you want us to follow you home?" I asked. As if!

"No, I'm going to Peter's house," she said.

I smiled. I still hadn't locked the doors to the house. While I did that, something crazy hatched in my mind.

"Babe, I want you to go talk to Cindy for a minute," I said.

"Why?" Jason asked.

"Can you just do it?" I asked.

"No," he said. Why was he choosing now, of all times, to challenge me?

"I have to go get something. Please, just do me this favor," I said.

"You can't talk to Cindy now?"

"No, I'm busy," I said.

"This doesn't make any sense," he said.

"We have an untraceable pre-paid cell phone hidden under the side deck for emergencies. I need to go get it."

"What's with your phone?"

I sighed. I hadn't anticipated having to tell him my whole plan! "I want to call myself with the other phone and then plant it in Cindy's bag to see if she's really going to Peter's house or if she's part of this."

Jason's face flushed. "Didn't she just get thrown down a flight of stairs, or is there something else you need to prove she's not part of this?" he said.

"Are you going to help me out of this or what?" I asked.

He was silent. I ran to get the cell phone. When I came back, he was in his car and Cindy was pulling away. I stared him down, but he wouldn't look at me. I was furious. I couldn't stop pacing back and forth in the front yard. He had just thwarted Plan A. What were we going to do? I was planning on getting some counter-intelligence with that plan. Now how would we find out what the enemy was up to? I walked to the passenger side car door. I felt like I was going to explode. Who gave him a right to do that? Had he seen what I had seen—Cindy hobnobbing with the enemy! No!

He got out of the car and slammed the door. He leaned over the roof. "Get in the car," he said.

"No."

www.UndercoverStarlet.com

"Are you going to walk wherever it is you plan on going?"

"Why did she drive away?"

"I told her I was taking you straight to your grandmother's house, and she seemed relieved."

"And you believed that?"

"She is your best friend. Why would you turn on her?" he asked.

I jumped into the car. He didn't get in the car immediately. When he did get in, I could see he was a bit steamed. He started the engine and pulled away without one word.

"Like you know where we're going," I said.

"Are you going to tell me?" he asked.

I wanted to ignore him. Just to make a statement. But we didn't have time for all that. Especially since he was driving, and I hadn't exactly figured out where we should go yet.

"You have problems, you know that?"

"I saw her talking in the bushes to the girl in the white hat," I said.

Jason rolled his eyes. "Forget that! I know you wouldn't believe that," he said.

"How could I not believe what I saw?" I said.

"You're too smart for that," he said.

"Uh, I know but ..." I started.

Then, suddenly, the moment he braked at the red light, he kissed me. I pulled away first. We drove for the next sixty seconds in silence. That kiss was kind of yummy.

"No more arguing, no more complaining. Tell me where you want to go," he said.

Chapter 10

An hour later, I was prepared to rock out my role as Bonnie, when I let my Clyde lead the way through the mall to the coffee house. I was ready for a shakedown—though I hadn't gotten around to telling Jason exactly why we were there and who we were looking for. There was too much daydreaming and kissing going on before we could even make it out of the car. On the escalator up to the second floor, I'd had to clear my mind.

There was only one person we could count on to rat out our opposition, and that was the wrongfully accused Roger. The coffee house was jumping with high school kids, a few from our school. There were a few college girls with their school sweatshirts on, pretending to meet about some class. But I could hear their whispers. They were secretly dishing on guys in their dorms. I guess that would be me next year.

The coffee house was nothing unusual, your typical commercial coffee place with a standard layout, lots of tan and brown colors everywhere, a few coffee beans up on the wall, quasi-comfortable chairs sparsely scattered about, and too many versions of espresso to count.

"Are you going to get something?" Jason asked.

"Yeah. That and prowl around for Cindy and Roger." They were probably sitting in some corner hiding behind the cover of the business section, all three feet of the town's clumsy, double-folded newspaper.

Jason got in line to order. "Don't worry, I got this."

"Okay. Meet me in the back with a mocha latte extra foam, babe." I felt bad not telling him the whole plan, but I needed to wait and investigate further before the big reveal, seeing as how Plan A was a complete bust.

I couldn't stop smiling while I checked every crevice for a multicolored, checkered shirt. So this was kinda like our first date. I mean he did pick me up. We'd had our first kiss, second, third, and well ... hmm. He had tried to save me from danger, and now he was ordering our first lattes together.

Aha! There was a guy. He was kind of on the lanky side. He was wearing a solid black T-shirt, reading a motorcycle magazine. Though none of this fit the scenario I had in my head, I had to check out all the leads. I had checked almost every inch of the place. This was the only possibility so far. I tried to mysteriously pull up a chair to his table. But the chair I selected had something stuck to the bottom of its legs. When I pulled it over to the table, it knocked and squeaked the whole way.

"Five-dollar lattes, and they can't afford to get a decent chair," I complained under my breath. So much for making a stealthy entrance. The guy sitting across from me slammed the bike magazine onto the table to reveal a short Caesar haircut, clean, dark, arched eyebrows and ... contacts. But he looked like Roger! He was a much better-looking, clean-cut version.

"Roger?" I hissed as if I'd suddenly discovered he was the secret evil villain in a fairy tale.

Apparently that wasn't the reaction he was after. From the look in his eyes I could see that the virtuous, sweet Roger had left the building.

"What the heck are you doing here? Two hours! I've been sitting here like a statue for two hours waiting for her. And she bailed on me," he said.

"Ummm." I wasn't sure what to tell him. I wasn't going to lie for Cindy.

"What are you? The messenger?" he asked. Since when did Roger operate on a short fuse? Things were all so very wrong. It was like the full moon was causing people to go mad.

Where was Jason with my sugary latte? I didn't have a plan, but if I did have one I would've scrapped it anyhow. This was completely unexpected and not in the thrilling kind-of-make-you-blush way. In the blink of an eye, Roger had turned into a metrosexual!

"Roger, what happened to you?" I asked.

"Oh, please stop whispering like this is the goddamn CIA," he said.

This was something out of a cartoon, in which the innocent baby in the stroller opens his mouth and starts talking like a beer-guzzling thirty-year-old. Roger took a look at the large black coffee he'd been nursing. He knocked back the last couple of sips in one gulp, like it was a shot.

"Don't worry. I'm not with them. I'm part of MIA," he said.

"MIA?" I said. I knew he wasn't trying to play me with my life on the line. "You listen and listen well." I leaned in close to him like one of those TV police interrogators. "I defied the police's orders and ducked my mom, who is traveling cross-country on a red-eye all because of this nonsense. Frankly, I don't care what kind of metamorphosis you've gone through. I came to get my life back. I want to know who's at the top," I said.

"Why? Your best friend didn't tell you?" he asked.

"She named a name. But I need more. I want you to name a name. And then I'm going to ask you for an address. It's plain and simple," I said.

Roger leaned back in his chair and pulled out a cigar. "Mind if I light up?" he asked. I snatched that damn cigar right out of his mouth.

"This is a latte bar, not a sleazy joint off some dingy, beaten route someplace. And, no, it is not cool to smoke. Haven't you seen those lung cancer commercials in which the people have to breathe through a hole in their neck?"

"No. I'm not allowed to watch television on weeknights," he said.

"I don't have time for this nonsense. Cough up the info, and hurry up."

Roger looked at his watch. Then he moved his coffee cup from the left side of the table to the right. I was trying my best to be patient. But when I saw him twiddling his thumbs, it was the last straw.

"Do I look like I'm here on a date? I came for the information! So give it to me," I said.

Now why did I have to go and say that? Maybe subconsciously I wanted to be alone for the rest of my natural life.

"No one would mistake this for a date," the sexiest voice on earth said from behind me. "Your extra-foam mocha latte." Jason dropped my coffee on the table in front of me. A piping-hot drop flew onto Roger's face.

"You will pay for that," Roger threatened.

"See, babe, this is Roger. He thinks he had a date with Cindy," I said.

"Didn't she say she was going to see Peter?" Jason winked at me to let me know he was playing along.

Roger's breathing started to get heavy. His eyes enlarged. Oddly, I still didn't find him remotely scary.

"What is MIA, anyway?" I asked.

Roger looked at Jason cockeyed. He gritted his teeth and shook his head. It was painstakingly apparent he didn't want to spill the beans.

"Look, Roger, give up the information," Jason said.

"I wouldn't be here if I really didn't need to know," I said. For a second I could see a glimmer of the old, compassionate Roger.

Roger threw his hands out and knocked his black coffee all over the table. Jason used the napkins he had in his hands to clean it up.

"I'll get some more napkins," I said.

"I can get them," Jason said.

"No, I'll get them." Roger jumped out of his seat and bolted for the door. Jason and I looked at each other. I speed-walked out of the shop and caught up with Roger on his way to the escalator. I grabbed his arm.

"What's the deal, Roger?" I asked. Roger scanned the area. He eyed every person on the escalator. Then he grabbed my arm and led me down the restroom hallway.

"I shouldn't tell you this, but I know you're clean. However ..." he said.

"What?" I asked.

"For reasons I cannot say, I could not tell you in front of the *basketball player*."

"Can you tell me now?"

"Mathlete Investigation Association."

"MIA you mean?"

"Uh, you call yourself a member of the National Scholars Association?"

Apparently I wasn't nerdy enough for Roger. "So, you're still a nerd?" I asked. There was hope. Everyone hadn't gone crazy.

"I prefer 'academically enhanced'."

I saw Jason out of the corner of my eye past the dimly lit restroom hallway. He was probably looking for me. I moved into a part of the corridor where we could not be seen.

"Roger, we get the same grades. Cut the act. What is with this look?"

"I, too, care about prom. I, too, need a prom date. Is there a need to spell it out?"

Jason walked past the corridor again in the opposite direction. Since we were in the basement of the mall there was no cell phone reception. I would have to go find him soon.

"Tell me now. I have to go. Who is at the top of the popular society?"

"What do I get out of this?"

"I have someone that might be able to go with you to prom."

"Promise?"

"I can't promise you a date, but looking like this you shouldn't have a problem getting a date if you drop the fake bad-boy act and just be the same nice guy you were."

www.UndercoverStarlet.com

"You think so?"

"I wouldn't have said it if I didn't think so," I said.

"Thanks." Roger smiled.

"The info?" I asked.

"The brains of the operation is Michelle," he said.

"I knew it! What is her address?"

"Ten-Ten Forelawn, right off Coldwell."

I hugged Roger. "Thanks!"

He acted a little shaken—like he had never been touched by a girl before or something. I started to run down the hallway.

"One more thing," he yelled.

I stopped cold in my tracks.

"There's just this one other thing. ..." His hands were shaking. "Cindy ..." he whispered.

"Cindy?"

"She's co-president of the society."

"Nia!" Jason called for me at the end of hallway.

My worst fear had materialized. I ran to Jason. Why did it seem like everything was so different in each moment? Plus, now Jason believed in Cindy as my friend. I couldn't bring myself to tell him.

"Why were you hiding here?"

"I wasn't hiding! I got the info we need," I said. He looked at me suspiciously.

"Babe, I had to follow him. We've come too far to just let him bolt out of the coffee shop. Now I know our next stop,"

I continued.

Jason put his arm around me. It felt good to know at least somebody had my back. "So how did you get him to tell you?" Jason asked.

"I threatened to turn my boyfriend loose on him if he didn't give me what I needed," I said.

"That's crazy. Did you really say that?" he asked. I didn't know what to say. I just raised an eyebrow. "'Cause that's kind of hot." He kissed my neck.

I tapped him on the butt. "Stay focused!" I said.

We had places to go and people to expose! One item was all an undercover starlet needed to even the score. And I had it: My trusty camera phone with voice recorder was going to save the day. It all seemed so simple in my head.

www.UndercoverStarlet.com

Chapter 11

In the car on our way to Forelawn my mother called. "My mother's plane lands in ten minutes," I said.

"What kind of flight was she on?"

"Well, it's almost ten. A nonstop would take about that time to get back to Long Island," I said.

"So we have ten minutes," he said.

"Basically. My grandparents' place should only be a couple of minutes from here," I said. I dialed my grandmother. "Hi, Nana, I'm on my way home. I had to take care of something. ... I'm fine. ... I know. I have to go. ... Okay ... I will. Bye."

"What do we want from her?" Jason asked.

"Answers! Like when this is this going to be over and why," I said.

When Jason opened my car door, he looked a little worried.

"What? I can take her," I said.

He laughed.

"I like that."

"You like what?"

"Your laugh. It's real. You know sometimes people laugh, but it doesn't feel like they really think it's funny," I said.

"So you like to keep it real," he said.

"Always." I smiled.

We approached the gate, me and my soldier. Out of nowhere, my cell started beeping. Cindy had sent me a text message.

"Don't do anything stupid. Things are complicated now, but they are going to stop. I am not home so don't go to my house unless you climb through my room window," she texted.

What was the prospect of that happening?

"Turn your cell phone off," I told Jason.

"I'll put it on silent," he said.

"Good idea." I put mine on silent too.

We walked around the house; there was no one outside.

"What if we just walked up to the front door?" Jason asked.

"No! I never saw James Bond doing that," I said.

"I think you might be wrong," he said.

I was so caught up in trying to figure out if he was calling me wrong, I didn't even notice him leading me by the hand up the grand, rolling driveway entrance. We walked right through the front door into the foyer of an old, Hollywood-style mansion. I hated Michelle, but what made it even worse was that her house was gorgeous.

"I can't believe that just worked," I whispered.

"I know." Jason popped the collar on his polo shirt.

I laughed under my breath. We stood there asking to be noticed while we pondered our next move.

"*Señora* Michelle," a short Hispanic woman called from the back of the house.

Jason and I ducked into what looked like a formal dinning room with a marble-top dining table for ten. The interior designing was impeccable. Who cared? We had to get out of there and allay this stalking issue. The woman's voice grew closer. We retreated to the back of the room. Jason quietly opened the door to the kitchen.

"There's no one in here. Come on."

He went, and I followed. The stark whiteness of the kitchen kind of freaked me out, and then there were spotlights everywhere! We ducked below the counters. I looked up for a minute and spotted a door at the back of the kitchen. The woman we had seen earlier came through the dining room door.

"Michelle!" she yelled.

She was dressed in a maid's uniform, holding a tray of those little finger sandwiches that didn't have any crusts. We scrambled around to the breakfast bar and hid underneath it. Jason peeked out over the ledge. I looked through the gaping entrance to the living room. Anyone coming from that direction could've spotted us a mile away. The maid cracked that lone door in the back. "I have sandwiches, Michelle," she said in a heavy Spanish accent.

"Bring them down," Michelle yelled.

Jason put his hand out for me to hold. "We're going to wait for her to come up, and then we'll go down," he said.

"Maybe we should hide in the dining room," I said.

I mean, who were we kidding? We weren't hiding from anyone with the 1,000 watts of light hitting us from every angle. We scurried across the kitchen back to the refuge of the dark dining room.

"Let's just get under here in case anyone comes in," I pointed to the table.

"I have to see her come back up," he said.

"Right."

What was going on? Wasn't I supposed to be leading this mission? I couldn't be too mad though, his idea did make sense. Jason cracked the door open. A sliver of light shined through the room. He kept one eye on the housekeeper. I watched the entrance to the foyer.

"Okay, she went in the living room," he said.

"Showtime," I said.

Next thing I knew, we were creeping down a narrow staircase. Jason quietly walked down a couple more stairs. He kneeled down a little until he could get a full view of what was going on. First he stared starry-eyed, then he squinted. He stood tall in front of me with his eyes glued to the floor. I could see he was carefully searching for the right words.

"Let's just bounce," he whispered in my ear.

What? I hadn't just crawled under some foreign dining room table and ducked the housekeeper to just up and go. Please! The part of me that was leading this mission was trying to be strong. I took a deep breath.

"Not today," I said.

He put his arms out and held onto the banister firmly so I couldn't get past him. I tugged at his arms as hard as I could.

"Are you for real?" It was becoming increasingly difficult to whisper. My temper was flaring up.

"Chill. Listen for minute. Sometimes, things look like one thing, but they're something else," he said.

"Don't I get a little more out of my fortune cookie? Tell me some words in Chinese."

I could see he was doing everything he could not to laugh. So I took another tug at his arm with no luck.

"Okay. You can stop grabbing me now," he said.

"Like you don't like it," I retorted.

He moved his hands from the stair rail to my waist as I crept past him to get an eyeful of the action. He lifted me up and placed me on the exact step he was on, as if I would see things the same way he did from there. He continued to hold onto me. I slowly ducked my head down to peek through the space between the banister posts.

I'm not sure which came first, my mouth dropping or the feeling of tears weighing down my lower lids. I know I had known it, but to see it felt like a stab in the chest—now I knew how Caesar felt. Uh! That AP English reading had me all discombobulated, thinking of all types of conspiracy theories.

She was like my sister. I ripped Jason's hands off me. All of a sudden I was Wonder Woman. I flew down the stairs and practically leapt my way over to the pool table where Michelle and Cindy stood. At this point, the wow factor of this glamorous farmhouse didn't faze me. The marble floors in the basement and the hand-painted mural on the ceiling were all part of Michelle's image. See, it would seem like someone who lived here should be above this whole stalking thing. But we all knew her cards.

As I approached, I could see Cindy handing Michelle the Dare Go Undercover bag I had been begging her for three months. And it was so unlike me to beg! Pleading is not my look. It was a StarletShop.com limited edition, for Christ's sakes. As if her betraying me and secretly cavorting with my enemy wasn't enough!

"I guess you took one for the team, getting your leg all bruised up and everything."

"No!" Cindy said.

I stood a couple of feet away from the best friends. Cindy had an iced latte in her hand, and she was notorious for throwing coffee on people. In junior year, she and Jane had gotten into a heated debate over some gossip about Cindy's latest boyfriend that Jane ran in the morning texts. It made it seem like he went both ways. Suddenly the supersize chocolate coffee Cindy had been drinking was all over Jane's face. I had no time for that. If she poured coffee on me, there would be no going back.

"Can't get enough of me, huh?" Michelle said.

My word, she was like that psycho from *Fatal Attraction*. Inside of that unbalanced mind of hers, we all wanted a piece of her.

"What are you doing?" Cindy whispered to me.

"Blowing this wide open!"

"Just let it ride. It's over. I got it. Go home," Cindy said.

"Right. What, are you two swapping your favorite finds? All this time! This is the depths of deceit."

I was so upset I didn't even think I was making any sense, but she knew what I meant. That was the thing about a best friend—they knew you. They knew what you meant and how you felt even when you were too angry to articulate your feelings. I was torn between wanting to cry tears of anger and wanting to choke Michelle.

"Stop following me! You will not come to my house anymore. This whole thing is so over," I said.

"Whatever do you mean?" Michelle giggled under her breath.

"Just shut up for freakin' once." Cindy grabbed Michelle by the shirt collar. "It is over. Just freakin' admit it so we can all go home, because if you scratch me again I will cut you!" Cindy continued.

"Get out! All of you! Including you, Jason. Vala, get back to work." Michelle looked right through me, over my shoulder.

When I turned around, what did I see? Jason, tucked away in a corner near the bottom of the stairs talking to a girl I'd never really seen around before.

"It seems like you want everything I've got. My ex-boyfriend, my ex-best friend, my picture in the yearbook. Do you want to double as me too?"

I drew a long breath as I racked my brain for more clever things to say. I was so angry my hand was twitching. It took everything in me to keep from slapping Michelle. One part of me figured there was no reason to be civil at this point. The other part of me said to just walk away. So I did. I had nothing left. I was running on empty. I couldn't believe Cindy. I had never been let down so much in my entire life.

"Did he tell you he's a member?" Michelle shouted.

Everyone in the basement stopped in their tracks. My eye caught Jason's. He stood up and knocked his head on the low ceiling by the staircase. Was this house made for midgets or just people under six-foot-four?

"I'm not in it. I never went to a meeting or anything. It's just part of being on the team."

"So that's what Roger meant when he said he couldn't tell me in front of the 'basketball player.'"

In a matter of hours, everything I had known was gone. So I did what anyone ex-popular girl in my shoes would've done. I walked up to Cindy and snatched that Undercover Starlet™ bag right off the table. She owed me at least that. I stormed past Jason, up the stairs. I realized things would continue on as they were without me. The juniors would finish working on the yearbook, Cindy would continue to be shallow, and I would always be the outsider with the worst luck with guys. But one thing would change. Even if Michelle decided to come after me again, mystery was not in her arsenal. The cat was out of the bag, and I was ready to go toe to toe with her. I could sense that she knew it too. The only question was: How was I going to get home?

"You don't want her either," Michelle said to Jason.

"Don't act like you know me. This is the second time I've talked to you since I've even been at this school," he said.

"Third," Michelle corrected him.

"At least she didn't come after you with a mask on and send strange notes and write things on the wall. You're sick! Then you took a sucker hit at Cindy and threw her down the stairs. Stay away from Nia if you know what's good for you!" Jason said.

"And I'm taking all my freakin' stuff back. I run half of this! So maybe you should be afraid." Cindy snatched up her things.

What? Was she trying to buy peace with her accessories? Please!

I tripped on the top step. As I fell forward, I felt two arms reach out and grab me, pulling me toward a warm body.

"I got you. I need you in one piece for prom," he said.

"Is that what you need?" I pulled his arms from around me.

"We don't have to rush. Just take your time," he whispered to me even though I was out of his reach. It was as if he knew I was listening out for him.

It angered me that he seemed to know just how I was feeling. I had that fight-or-flight thing going on. I was either going to wring someone's neck or run. I hurried to the door. I practically slid across the floor. When I reached the door, I stopped. I didn't know why, but for some reason I couldn't leave. Not like that.

"So who was she?"

I was jealous. Even I hadn't realized it until the words floated right out of my mouth. If this was just lust or infatuation, would I be jealous? I didn't even know if I was the possessive type. I'd only been in one relationship, if you could call it that.

He drew his lips together as if they had been pulled together by a drawstring. He thought hard. He reached past me and grabbed the doorknob. "Let me get that so we can go," he said.

"We? Here I am confronting this witch who's been making my life a living hell, and you're getting your rap on with some girl!"

"Whoa! I think you need to bring that down a notch. And maybe we could leave before we argue," he said.

"No."

"Well, first off, I wasn't tryin' to talk to her. Second, I was asking her why Cindy was giving Michelle money," he said. I turned away from him. "Do you still want to talk about this in here?" he asked.

I waited and waited for him to turn the doorknob. The hairs on the back of my neck stood up as I felt his breath on the back of my neck. He was in no rush to open that door. I think he was smelling my hair.

"So when are you going to be gone?" Michelle asked. Her voice was most unpleasant, so scratchy and sour-sounding.

"Don't turn around," Jason said.

I didn't. I even surprised myself. Normally, I would've lashed out at him attempting to control me, but somehow it felt more like he had my back.

The door was slammed behind us. This was all turned around. It was nothing like the way I thought it would be. I was supposed to be the one with the attitude. I was the one who was supposed to emerge as the victor. Yet somehow it felt like the tables had been turned. This wasn't about some damn yearbook photo, that was for sure! I had come too far. Plus, I had dragged Jason into this.

Michelle couldn't just go around thinking she could screw around with anyone she wanted to. There were codes to live by. People were entitled to live in peace. I was tired of her being all up in my space disturbing my peace. Though I was sure Jason would sleep well tonight, resolution or not, I wouldn't. It was high time I had the final word, not some punk-ass freak—even that description was too courteous for that deranged witch. No one should have to look over her shoulder in her own house—except maybe her.

"So what did she say?" I asked.

"About Cindy?" he asked.

www.UndercoverStarlet.com

I nodded my head, yes.

"She just said Cindy and Michelle were arguing about you before we came in. Then I asked what they were doing, and she said they were laying out the yearbook. I asked her to make sure that we were in."

I knew he was just saying "we" so I wouldn't feel alone in this stalking boat. He would have no problem getting his picture in the yearbook, especially the way that girl was looking at him. She wanted him for breakfast and maybe seconds for lunch. Even I didn't look at him like that ... yet.

At the curb, I had to leave him behind.

"I'm coming," he contested.

"No, because both of us will be caught. Something is not right! I just feel like I have to see her room. Something tells me that if I get into her head a little, I can turn this around."

"So you're not the type of girl to leave well enough alone?"

"I thought you might've figured that out back at the door—while you were deciphering my conditioner scent, that is."

He wandered past me toward his car. I think he felt a little embarrassed. I had to cough to keep from laughing.

"I'll call you when it's over," I said.

"All right, I'll be here at my car."

"I'm a big girl. I'll be okay."

"You handle your biz. Call me, text me, or whatever if you need me."

"I can take care of myself."

"You're kind of feisty, though."

"Are you scared for her or for me?"

"I definitely am not scared for you." He laughed. It was weird.

"What is it?" I asked.

"You're the only girl I know who would do this."

"I have no choice. It has to be done!" I could see a smile in his eyes. "You like that, huh?" I asked.

He licked his lips. "Don't let this stupid chick get in your head. 'Cause you are much bigger than her," he said.

It was like he was almost proud of me for standing up for myself. I felt like a better person around him.

"You're special." I started to walk away immediately. How could I have said that? He pulled me back to him. Oh man, I wish it was like a phone call that I could abruptly hang up or in which I at least could make up an excuse to go.

"I, I have to go. It's ... getting late."

Somewhere between my brain and my mouth words were getting lost for no reason. Sometimes when he touched me, my mind just went haywire.

"All right. Me, in the car waiting for you. And ... yeah, I might feel the same way. I think you're kind of special," he said. He abruptly turned around. I watched him walk to his car, but I didn't want him to know it.

I walked slowly back to the house, thinking about him the whole way. I wanted to turn around to see his face again. But the chance that he was watching me and would see me look back at him was pretty high—80, maybe 90 percent. Gosh! This was crazy. This is what happened when an over-thinker fell in love.

I had to shake off this Jason stuff and focus. This time, I was really going to kick in some spy techniques. I wondered if I'd have to scale a wall to her bedroom. I crept around the side of the house doing the obligatory 007-style scoping and probing about the scene bit. I spotted a window to the upstairs hallway, right next to what looked like Michelle's bedroom—unless she had a younger sister that had teddy bears in the window. Anyway, I needed to operate surreptitiously. Entering a window was the best bet. I was looking for a window to a room somewhere that someone wouldn't be sitting in. A hallway would do. How auspicious! There was an old tree right by the upstairs hallway window, which was right next to the window that had all the teddy bears.

Using one leg and then the other, I climbed that tall tree to the highest second-story window on earth. I hadn't climbed a tree since I was seven. And I didn't have fond memories of that but I did have a scar on my arm to remember it by. What the heck was I thinking? I reached out almost three feet between the tree limb and the window. I didn't dare look down. I knew better than that. One look down and I might've freaked out and toppled to the ground. Next thing you know, I'd wake up to Michelle's face laughing over my broken body.

Unexpectedly, I was able to just slide the window up and open. Does anybody lock anything around here? This is New York! At my house, we practically have a padlock on every window except the basement, which I didn't know about until today.

I slid through the window head first. At this point, I didn't care if anyone did see me. My whole body was making it into that window. There was no way I was going to leave any part of me dangling outside. The mere thought creeped me out.

There I was in the middle of the hallway, practically face-down. I could tell that the muscles in my arms and shoulders would be hurting in the morning. Climbing through that window was like doing fifty push-ups. A hand helped me up. The first thing I noticed were the Fred Flintstone-style, open-toed, dollar-store slippers that the round-bellied, five-foor-five little boy had on.

"Hey, you. I've seen you before?" he whispered.

Where? At Chucky E. Cheese? He was, like, twelve. I stood up and made my way to Michelle's room.

"Is she in there?" I asked. He shook his head, no. I slid the super-mod frosted-glass door back, prepared for a confrontation.

I stood there scoping out her room. There were like fifteen teddy bears on the window seat. A huge sultan bed and a powder area, and the color scheme was lavender and electric blue. Surprisingly, they went very well together. Of course she had a canopy bed and double doors that looked like they led to the holy grail of walk-in closets. She had a pair of skis in the corner. I could feel my blood pressure going up. I had spent four years fantasizing about going skiing with my boyfriend. Just before Craig—the only black guy I knew who liked to ski—and I were going to go cross country-skiing, Michelle had intercepted. One might see how I found myself grinding my teeth at the sight of those skis. I felt a short, rounded object poke me in the gut. I looked around to find this little boy at my side again. I stared at him for a moment.

"Hurry up," he said.

"Excuse me?" I said.

"You're very pretty," he said.

"Who are you?" I asked.

"Leonard," he said. Was I supposed to care what his name was?

"Why are you here?" That was a better question. Sometimes

www.UndercoverStarlet.com

you had to ask the right question to get the right answer.

"Follow me." He opened the doors to the mini-loft of a walk-in closet. Every designer outfit from every teen magazine printed that year alone hung in that closet. Each outfit was perfectly matched together with accessories—handbags, tights, shoes, and bangles. It was like she had a personal stylist. I lost him somewhere at the second turn around the spinning clothing rack of dark rinse jeans.

"C'mon! She may be back." His voice cracked slightly. He cleared his throat and continued to talk in a faux-deep voice. "Look here."

He pulled back five different styles of white, cotton button-down blouses to reveal a tack board full of pictures … of me! Correction, me in eighth grade? Even I don't look at pictures of me in eighth grade. This was completely ridiculous and wrong. Very, very wrong. I mean, who has a collage of pictures of another girl from eighth grade, uh … and tenth grade? There were a couple of pictures of me in the eleventh grade, too. This was officially my worst nightmare. I had never felt so violated and furious in my life! She had a picture of me and Craig ripped down the middle and taped back together! And then my half was cut into shreds.

It's one thing if I ripped up a picture, but this was like some witchcraft stuff. Man, the average person sheds like 100 hairs a day. I'd been in and out of this house twice already, and at least ten of my hairs were lurking around somewhere. What would she do with them? Hold some kind of ritual? I made the sign of the cross across my chest and hightailed it out of there.

Of course I found the sliding doors closed. That was strange, unless Leonard had closed them. And where had that little leprechaun gone anyway? Had he abandoned ship? I tried to quietly slide the doors back but Michelle had my number.

She was on the other side. She yanked me by the arm out into the hallway. I pushed her off me. I was so freaked out that she would be collecting sample hairs off my shirt, I didn't want her touching me.

"What were you doing in there?" she snarled.

"Afraid I saw your altar full of my pictures?" I asked.

"That is not an altar!"

"Denying it does not somehow make it sane!"

There would be no reasoning with someone like her. I brushed past Michelle. I was heading to the front of the house. I just wanted to get out of there. She jumped in front of me.

"April 5, 2003. I was minding my business, trying to return sour milk. You accused me of trying to cut the line and called me Marshmallow Girl in front of the entire student body. I was a few pounds overweight or whatever. You were gross, and nobody nicknamed you. People called me Marshmallow Girl for the rest of junior high," Michelle said.

"Are you out of your mind? Get over it! That was how many years ago?"

"Ken Walker," Michelle said. Was this some sort of delusion?

"Who?" I said.

Suddenly she slammed me against the wall and had her forearm pinned under my chin. "I asked him to the Sadie Hawkins dance and you know what his friends said? He's waiting for Nia to ask him."

"Get off me."

I yanked her hair as hard as I could. She shrieked.

"I don't even remember this alleged guy and so chances are I didn't go anywhere with him. Sue me if he liked me and you liked him. We weren't even in the same class."

She let her arm down, and I turned her around and slammed her against the wall. "This psychotic obsession is going to stop tonight!"

"See, first I skipped a grade. We're in the same class now. Had you not taken four years to get a decent boy-friend, we could've met sooner."

"School is over in four weeks, get a life!"

"Oops! My bad! It took you four years to find any boyfriend at all!"

"I don't care what you say. If this is about revenge, you're not getting any,"

"My current job is to make your life miserable like you made mine. I couldn't get a boyfriend. I couldn't make friends. I was nobody, thanks to you! One cameo and you ruined my life!"

Michelle kicked me in the shin then took a swing at my jaw. I ducked back. That kick in the shin felt like someone was driving a nail through my leg.

"Did I mention I've been in kickboxing since seventh grade for my aggression and to keep the baby fat off?" she continued.

Her ranting on and on created the perfect opportunity. It took all the strength I had to ignore the mind-numbing pain radiating through my bone. I kicked her in the shin. She crouched down to the floor and swept her foot underneath me. I flew to the ground faster than I'd like to recall.

"The thing was, you weren't even popular and he liked you. Everything you did mattered. I am so sick of people like you! Now I'm a somebody, and I made you a nobody."

I jumped back up. "Five years, and you're still stuck in eighth grade! See a therapist, loser! This is not my problem! Stop sending me text messages and viruses! Now I know it's you sending me that stuff!" I backhanded her with my left hand. I just happened to be wearing this huge crystal ring. But it was too soon to claim victory. Her hand had passed across my face in the worst way.

"It was sweet, wasn't it? Hope your computer works," she said.

My face was burning. I could feel the welt forming on my cheek. She reached out to grab my throat. I poked her in the eyes with my two fingers. Her hand waved around my face as she tried to fight back with her eyes blinded. Leaving like this, knowing she'd harbored these ill feelings for so many years led me to be suspicious that she wouldn't leave me alone after this. I walked toward the front of the house to the stairs. I was still leaving without anything concrete. What if she moved that board when the police came to raid her house? The police raid was probably wishful thinking. In my mind, I hoped they would come with a paddy wagon for the insane and reel her away. This was not good sleuth work. Yet I felt compelled to get out before another cat fight ensued. Steps away from the top of the staircase, I was struck in the back of the head. I guess I should've been looking over my shoulder. Whatever she hit me with felt like a rock—much like the thing that beat inside her chest.

I don't know how many hours later it was, or maybe it was just twenty minutes. Somehow twenty minutes always felt like an hour. I was shaken awake by this tall, skinny guy from my AP English class. "You may not know it, but you have the most gorgeous hair I have ever seen."

What a great way to wake up—a guy wearing a computer

logo shirt, and thick glasses showering you with compliments while you're tied up. I started to try and wiggle my hands free. Seeing me struggling, after copping a feel of my hair, he finally untied the stockings that tied my hands together. I ripped the piece of Scotch tape off my lips. What the heck else had she done? Given me a barrage of paper cuts?

On second thought, I shouldn't joke like that. Paper cuts hurt more than gaping wounds, especially when they're on your hand. Such a scenario would be extremely excruciating for someone like me who washed their hands, like, fifty times a day.

"How did you get in here? The hallway window?" I asked.

"Secretly, underneath this computer science T-shirt I have an S on my chest and inflatable muscles," he said.

"What?" I was so confused. Was this actually happening, and why was he joking at a time like this?

"Ha! Girl, do I look like I can climb through a window?"

He had a point. I quickly stood up to find that she had me tied up underneath that freaky photo board. I shoved all the shirts back and took out my cell phone. *Click.* I jumped back a couple of steps for a panoramic picture. *Click.* And I took one more close-up.

"What are you doing?"

I studied his face. "Gary, right?" I asked.

He threw his hand up in the air as if he were about to testify. "That is I. Child, please tell me this chick has not made a suspect collage of you. This is like a missing person's timeline!"

Oh, my goodness! He watched crime show dramas too!

"Since we're under oath, I cannot lie," I said.

"Girl, I am so sick of Michelle. You know, she raided my house with her Neanderthal boyfriend and, of course, her sidekick. They gagged me!"

"What!" I said.

"Yes, they gagged me for a page in the yearbook. I'm here to stop that girl in her tracks and get my photos back. The last straw was when she stole my Internet ID."

"And I thought the dropkick was bad." I laughed. This whole thing was so preposterous, there was no other reaction more befitting.

At this point, I was scared of this psycho. I was sure she'd get some much-needed psychiatric help once I reported all of this to Detective Smart. Gary led me through the labyrinth of a closet. That bad boy had like 1,000 square feet. I couldn't understand why Michelle would spend her time obsessed on adolescent happenings when she had everything ... except a soul, that is.

"How did you know I was here?"

"This doll saw me in the kitchen and whispered to me to get you out of here."

"Did she say why?" Like being tied up underneath cut-up pictures of yourself in someone else's room wasn't reason enough.

"No. She was like 'Don't tell Michelle, and do it now while Michelle is in the basement. Be quick.' I knew she was on point because I heard 'witchee Michee' yelling at somebody about fonts," he said.

Gary poked his head out of the sliding door. He looked left, then right down the hallway. *"Psst."* Gary hissed. *"Psst!"* This time, he was a little louder.

www.UndercoverStarlet.com

My patience was wearing thin. I tried to peek through the sliding doors to see what he was doing. Leonard was trotting down the hall at a leisurely pace.

"Leonard!" I called out. He started to sprint down the hall like a triathlon athlete. I guess I still had an effect on grade school boys.

"How can I serve you?" he asked.

"We have to—" I said.

"What happened to your face?" Leonard cut me off.

"Shhh!" Gary said. I rushed over to the full-body mirror in the back of the room. Had she taken a sucker punch at me while I was out? Of all the things I'd gone through, this was the straw that broke the camel's back!

"Why didn't you say I had the remnants of a fist mark on my FACE?" I yelled at Gary.

"Child! Pipe down," he said.

I touched my pulsating eye socket. Funny how it hadn't been pulsating until now.

"Go look out for Michelle," Gary told Leonard.

"Are you leaving?" Leonard asked.

"Yeah," I said.

"You didn't have to crush his whole dream like that," Gary said.

"Will you be coming back?" Leonard asked as he stood post at the end of the hall.

"Please," I said.

"Why don't you take a picture of her for your screensaver and keep it moving," Gary said. Leonard ran up to me with his

Sidekick in his hand. Gary turned him about-face. "I was kidding. Go back and look out," he said.

"You never said what you were going to do now?" I said.

"Even the score," he said.

"Word," I said. I couldn't help but wonder if he was MIA. He fit the profile: nerdy, crazy, co-conspirator against Michelle's clan.

"I'll tell you once you get out," he said.

Gary quietly sprinted to the other end of the hall. He motioned me to come to him. This was like a prison. A door slammed at the opposite end of the hall.

"Oh, no," Gary said. I kept my back against the wall this time. I turned around, and the wicked witch was back. Michelle came thrashing down the corridor like a quarterback on Super Bowl Sunday. Gary hid around the corner—so much for getting even. Cowardice had a paralyzing effect, even on the quasi-brave.

I wasn't about to run. It was time we had a final showdown, and this time I was going to use my brains. She hurtled toward me with her hands fluttering every which way like she was ready for a cat fight. I threw a little acting into the bit.

"Oh no!"

And just when she jumped toward me, I jumped out of the way. Luckily, the hardwood floor broke her attempt at a tackle. I wasn't sure if she was pretending or what. So I kicked her in the belly to confirm. She didn't so much as whimper.

"She's out like a light," I said.

Gary returned from his corner slowly. "Child, you know I don't do fights," he said.

www.UndercoverStarlet.com

"Is that so?" I said sarcastically.

"I had to let you two handle your business," he said.

"Get her legs. And call Leonard," I said.

"Leonard!"

We dragged Michelle face-down into her bedroom. I hoped the Berber carpet gave her face rug burn.

"Yes?" Leonard came into the room dressed to the nines in a crisply ironed button-down shirt, jeans with the tags on, and fresh white kicks.

"Oh, God, what are you dressed up for?" Gary sighed under his breath.

"Come here. Get the doors," I said. He slid the bedroom doors closed. "Get a chair, Leonard. Gary, get those stockings she used to tie me up." They hurried back with the goods. "Let's get her up into the chair. Tie her arms behind the chair."

"Wha-at?" Gary said in a sing-song tone.

I stood there for a moment eyeing Michelle's limp body, trying to figure out what we were going to do with her. "What's the next step?" I asked.

"Was that rhetorical?" Gary asked.

"No!"

"Oh, don't get all crazy." I think we were half-past crazy already. "Take a picture of her," Gary suggested.

"Yes! And I know just who to send it to," I said.

I took out my trusty, lean, mean mobile phone machine. I started snapping away from all angles. I would select the worst for forwarding.

"Who are you sending it to?"

"The whole school."

"Who are you? Gossip Mafia?"

I looked Gary up and down. "What do you know about that?"

"We go to the same school—hello. Even I get the trickled-down gossip word."

"Believe me, I'm not the brains behind Gossip Mafia."

"Do the do. Send away. Let's sit her by the teddy bears. Leonard, you go get that creepy board with the pictures of her," he said.

"If we're going to put this in the morning text we need her to look more deranged so it makes the first paragraph," I said.

"Leonard, bring me the scissors," he yelled. A sinister smile crept on his lips. "Now this is my territory—haircuts," he continued.

These MIA guys were nuts. Leonard bowed his head when he brought Gary the scissors, as if he were paying his respects to Gary. Then he handed me the board.

Ten minutes later, I emailed Jane. High fives were in order all around.

"Good work, team!" I said.

"Goodie for that witch! But we should go before she wakes up," Gary said.

"Oh, I have just one more thing to take care of," I said.

On my way to the closet, I checked the full-body mirror. Well, the welts on my eye had finally gone down. But I couldn't forgive that easily. I scooped up that pair of skis into my hands. "Are you taking those?" Gary asked.

"Too conspicuous?" I said.

"I don't care. She probably doesn't even use those. Her family never goes skiing," Gary said.

I put the skis back down. In my mind, I was going to clock her one good time in the face with the back edge of the skis to leave a welt on her face like she had left on my face. An eye for an eye was what I wanted. But I had reached my mean threshold. Not that she didn't deserve a good whack in the face. Just because she was violent, though, didn't mean I had to be violent. In fact, I'd probably go my entire life without experiencing so much violence again. Hopefully!

"You better bounce soon," Leonard said.

I think spending too much time in Michelle's room with her being in there had him scared. Gary and I looked at each other and laughed. We walked out, and Leonard quietly closed the doors behind us. I broke that stalker board in half and took it with me. I'd kindly deposit it in the garbage at the curb.

"So what did you say in the text?" Gary asked.

"Vote for me for prom queen. You know you want to be me. XOXO Witchee Michee."

I giggled. Now it felt like it was finally over.

"You are so bad!" Gary said.

"Wait," I looked back, and Leonard was following us out. "Thanks for all of your help," I kissed Leonard on the forehead.

"Let's make like a banana ... and split," Gary said.

"I had such high hopes for you." I rolled my eyes. Split? Come on.

"Isn't that the coolest thing to say? Leonard says it

sometimes," Gary said.

"I do not," Leonard said.

"It's just so sad no one will know that was my work. I mean who else could do an asymmetrical bob in ten minutes?" Gary said.

He did have some guts. He had to have guts to cut a girl's hair six, maybe seven inches while she was knocked out cold.

"Yeah, we need to go a little faster," I said. Once Michelle saw that haircut, she was going to go ballistic.

"Lenny, call the 'rents and tell Aunt Beatrice that Michelle, um ... had a wild party in the basement and now she's all tied up in her bedroom and say you think they were drinking and stuff. Make sure you tell them she's unconscious," Gary said. Gary's eyes popped out of their sockets when he said the word "unconscious."

"Okay." Leonard ran away with a great, big smile.

"Now they'll rush home, halting yearbook production," he whispered slyly.

It was like Gary was another person. He even talked differently. He was in his element. Wow. To think we weren't even friends all this time. He was great. Cindy would've loved him.

"Tell Roger, thanks," I said.

"You know Roger?" he asked.

"What are you talking about? Don't you?" I asked.

"Yeah," he said.

"Yeah," I said. We walked down the stairs.

"I have some business downstairs with a certain doll face and my yearbook photos," he said.

www.UndercoverStarlet.com

"So you dig girls?" I said.

He flung himself against the banister and slapped his hand to his chest. Then in one snap second, he tripped down three steps backward and was really grasping the banister for dear life. Was that a yes?

"Do you think I should leave out this door?" I had my hand on the front door. But that wouldn't make for a stealthy exit.

"No, try the side door. That's how the maid puts out the garbage. It's almost always open, and no one would see you. I came in through there."

We walked through the kitchen. There was no hiding or no looking over our shoulders … well, okay, I looked over my shoulder once. After being knocked in the head, you might do that a few times. I sure felt big and bad though, like, "What! You want some of this!"

It was like my boyfriend said, no other girl would do this. So it sure felt good standing in my own shoes. It was like the weight of five men had been lifted off my shoulders. Now what five-foot-eleven 140-pound girl would hold five men on her shoulders? I didn't know, but metaphorically, yeah, that could be me.

www.CameoTheNovel.com

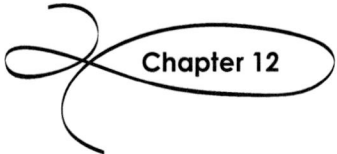

Chapter 12

Outside as sure as the sun rises every morning, there he was inside the Mustang parked right across the street, just where I'd left him. I ran up to the car and knocked on the window. He got out of the car.

"What happened?" he asked.

"You waited for me all that time?" I asked him.

He shrugged. "I gave my word," he said.

"You didn't leave for a minute? Not even to get food?" I asked.

"Nah," he said.

"So this was like a stakeout for you," I said.

"I played solitaire and listened to my iPod," he said.

I laughed. My gentleman opened the door for me. As I watched him walk around the car I knew this would be the last time in a long time I'd ride shotgun with him. It was half-past twelve on a weeknight!

"So what happened?"

"I'm so over talking about Michelle. You know I took care of business," I said.

"That's my girl."

I turned the radio on.

"Where do your grandparents live?"

He turned on the ignition.

"Let's just wait a minute," I said. I kissed him. "You know you're like my angel. I can't believe you really waited for me all this time," I said.

"I was going to go inside. I kept calling you to see what was going on, but I figured you would come out sometime. I know you weren't about to stay there overnight. A few more minutes, though, and I would've called the detective," he said.

I put my seat back. "Open the sun roof. There's a full moon out," I said.

He put his seat back too.

"Is it past your curfew?" I asked.

"Yeah, but I called my people."

"Your people?"

"Yeah, the people who own the house I live in."

"Oh, those people."

"Yeah, I told them I was helping a friend out. My mom was kind of worried, but I told her that my friend just needed a ride home. She asked me if you needed help. See, my whole family got your back." Guys always had a habit of extrapolating the truth.

"I just want you to have my back," I said.

"Yes, sir!" he said.

"Good. I like that," I said.

We held hands and watched the moon and the stars for a minute. It had been so long since I had looked at the Big Dipper.

Life was so much more complicated than looking at the

stars. Who would've thought I would ever be here? In my mind, he was the guy who'd never called, but that had all changed this week.

"Can't we just stay here all night?" I said.

He laughed. "Avoiding going home?" he said.

"Somehow, if I arrive home at 6 a.m. versus 1 a.m. I think my punishment will be much worse."

"I agree."

I wiped my lip gloss off his full lips. "We have to make a right at the corner and take that street for about ten blocks."

"Let's burn out then."

"Now, don't go too fast. No rushing."

"I got this. And I wouldn't rush." Were we still talking about driving home?

I told myself I wouldn't talk until we got there. With boys, less was always more. And I had him just where I wanted him. However, about halfway there, suddenly I had a change of heart. Who wants to ride for ten minutes without saying anything? Come on.

"I still can't believe this whole secret society thing escalated this far. It was completely out of hand," I said.

Jason cleared his throat. "You think this is the worst thing that could happen to you, don't you?" he asked.

"I'd say this ranks up there pretty high. Don't you?" I said.

"I know of things that could be worse," he said.

"Like what?" I asked.

"Last year, I was going out with this girl, Kelly." My Jason spoke of her as if his memory of her was quite vivid. The way he carefully selected his words when describing her had me wondering if he would one day describe me like that. "She had everything. She was smart, hilarious, and pretty. She was a nice person. Then, one day, it didn't matter," he said.

Maybe he had told me more than I wanted to know. I was feeling a little uncomfortable. I preferred to stay in my world. Kelly had recovered from a small nervous breakdown in her senior year of high school. She was one year older than us. She was about to finish her freshman year at college with a 3.8 GPA. Apparently they were still in touch. His tone told me that he had loved her. I couldn't help but wonder, no, maybe just hope he would love me. They had dated for two years and, toward the last six months, her family life had started to get really rough. Her parents got divorced and her mother started working three jobs to pay the bills. She had to watch her four little brothers and sisters all day after school and on weekends. "She was under all this pressure. Babe, even though things seem bad, they could be worse. And it can always get better," he said.

Compared to Kelly, he probably saw me as a bubble gum drama queen. I shrugged my shoulders.

"Are you okay?" he asked.

"Fine," I said.

What was happening to me was real, but compared to a nervous breakdown it was kind of petty. At least it seemed like that was where he was going with this conversation. I had been in at least three altercations that week alone! That wasn't light stuff in my book.

Part of me resented him. Yet part of me grew up a little bit. I didn't just like him. He saw things differently. He knew things I didn't know. He would love me differently. I didn't know everything there was to know about high school love or high school boys. I stopped thinking I had one up on him. I hadn't realized it, but I had thought I was better than him in some way. And I was wrong. He was a far cry from the fallacy of good looks and popularity.

I was breathing funny. My heart was pounding. It was the same car, I had on the same clothes, I even had on the same makeup, just slightly worn. There was no time to freshen up post-brawl. I didn't know how I looked to him. But through my eyes, I saw him so clearly for the first time. I had sat in that same seat all day. How could things feel so different in just a few hours? The way I saw him, I couldn't dare let him know.

All along, I thought I was courageous going after these secret society freaks, but that wasn't the real test. See, he had more courage than I did. It had been like this all along. I thought there were rules and games to play to keep him under wraps. At no time with him did I feel like I had to question how he felt about me. I never worried that if I said something stupid, he might text me to never call him again. Why had I come to this conclusion just now? I felt naked, in a way. Like there was something between us, a connection where he knew what I was feeling on some level. I quickly started to feel sick to my stomach. In my gut, I knew my inexperience was coming back to haunt me, rearing its ugly head in the form of insecurity. At a time like this, what was the best thing to do? Keep my mouth shut.

It took me some time to get out of the car, though he stood there with the door open for a while. I was unsettled. He wasn't a cameo in my life. And I didn't want another. But it was our song, wasn't it?

"Are you okay?" he asked.

I just looked at him. No words could form upon my lips.

I walked past him to the gate. He walked by my side. He took hold of my hand. It took me a minute to decide if I should grab his tightly. It felt like he could see me, see inside me, and he would know how I really felt about him. There was a little voice in my head screaming, "Don't show your cards!" In the blink of an eye, I was head over heels.

I caught a glimpse of my grandmother's eyes looking disapprovingly through the slightly drawn curtain in the front window. But I didn't care what Jason and me coming home at 1 a.m. looked like. I stopped at the stairs leading to the door.

"It's late. You better go in. I hope you don't get in too much trouble, babe," he said.

"If I can't call you until graduation because my cell phone has been repossessed, wait for me. Won't you?" I asked.

"You don't have to ask."

"Thanks for the ride home."

What I really wanted to say was "Thank you for giving a real damn about me." He made me want to shower him with hugs and kisses again and again. You know, sometimes we fall, but the important thing is that we get back up, dust ourselves off, and get back in the dating game to win. All of the pieces of me felt like I had won.

"I'll see you tomorrow at school, out front, 8 a.m.," he said.

It was the first time in a long time I was actually looking forward to school the next day. He kissed me on the cheek.

"I like that." I didn't want him to go.

"If beauty was complicated and crazy and it had to be

personified as a person, it would be you," he said with a triumphant smile.

"Was that a compliment?" I asked.

He blushed a little. I think it was the first time he'd been embarrassed in front of me—maybe the second.

"See, I think you're beautiful, but I couldn't think of a way to say it and not sound corny."

"Being beautiful is never corny, not even in soap operas."

I mean he was the only guy that could pull off "babe" without sounding kind of sugary, so corny was nothing for him. He could definitely pull off "beautiful." For the rest of the night, I'd be replaying that moment in my head. I watched him walk away anyway. He turned back to me and waved. I broke out in a smile from ear to ear. Boy, was he everything! Somehow this guy had gotten a hold on my heart. And I liked that.

Oh gosh! I was so embarrassed at how I liked him. Nothing that happened now could seem so bad, except maybe my angry mother.

Chapter 13

When I got inside I was expecting to have to duck. I didn't really know how angry my mother would be. I quietly closed the front door behind me. My grandparents had apparently recently renovated the first floor. It'd been so long since I had gone over there, I didn't even know. I couldn't dare turn the front hallway light on. Instead, I tripped over some strange built-in cabinet contraption they had erected just behind the front door.

Whatever. I had more important things to focus on. I took a deep breath as I leaped toward the staircase.

"Nia!" my grandmother whispered from the top of the stairs.

I was so startled I nearly fell backward down the stairs. When I looked at her, she pointed down the hall.

"Sorry, Nana," I whispered.

"Baby, don't worry about me. Your mama's waiting for you in your Stephen's old room. You better go," she said.

At the top of the stairs, I walked over to my grandmother and gave her a big hug and kiss. She was way cooler than I remembered.

The walk up the hallway to my father's old room seemed like eternity. I wondered if my father had gotten in trouble like this. When I stayed with him in the summer, he always told me stories of his crazy escapades. He was pretty mischievous. Me, I tried to mind my own business. Yet, somehow, I still ended up doing the walk of shame. It was inevitable that some form of punishment would ensue. But I had nothing to be ashamed of. I stood up for myself.

What was I going to say? I couldn't very well tell my mother exactly where I'd been and what I'd been doing. In teen movies they always make it look like parents understand us, but in real life they just grounded you for longer when you told the whole story. I was about to open the door when my mother fiercely swung it open for me.

"Come in, young lady. You're finally here! Uh! You were supposed to be here hours ago. Where were you?" she asked.

"I was out."

"What? I rushed to the airport. It cost over $1,000 extra for a flight change. Not once did you pick up your cell phone."

Once I started tuning my mother out, I noticed my father's room. I usually stayed in the guest bedroom when I stayed at my grandparents' house. I think I had only been in here once. It was great. There were model airplanes hanging from the ceiling, '70s basketball posters on the walls, and two half bunk beds. I guess my father and my uncle had shared a bunk bed.

"Nia! Are you listening?"

"Yeah,"

"We're going to have to go down to the police station tomorrow and get a police report. I haven't even gotten a chance to call Cindy's parents. Imagine! This is very disturbing."

"Mom, I know it's terrible and all, but it's over. I found out who was doing it, and I took care of it."

"You know your grandmother thought you would try

something like this. She said you probably went after whoever it was at the school who was bothering you," my mother said.

"She did?"

"Those were her exact words."

"She was right!"

"I wish you would've called. I was worried out of my mind, young lady."

"I'm sorry. I know I should've called."

"We'll talk about this more in the morning. Get some sleep." My mother walked out the door.

"Wait. In here?" I asked.

"Yes. Your grandmother thought you might want to sleep in here tonight."

"Why?"

"She said that you and your dad have a lot in common."

"Like what?"

"You're both rebellious."

"I am not rebellious."

"I think your grandmother thinks she's psychic. She also mentioned something about you getting married at a young age."

"Who?"

"Who knows? It's late."

When my mom had married my dad they were both around twenty-two. I was only seventeen! There was no doubt in my mind that my grandmother had gone nuts. You can't just think things up and call yourself a psychic.

"Good night, Mom. I love you."

"I love you, too."

I couldn't go straight to sleep. I had so much anxiety. It was already three or four hours past my normal bedtime. So much had happened in one night, I couldn't relax my mind. I kept thinking about this story my mother used to tell me. My mind was probably trying to forget my grandmother's so-called predictions.

It was an old fable about an African princess. She had to confront another kingdom to find out why their crops were missing. Every time they went into the field to pick their fruits and vegetables, many had already been plucked. The princess did not understand why. Everyone in her kingdom was well fed and very loyal. They were happy to be there, and she trusted them. So she knew it couldn't be anyone from her kingdom.

Upon confronting another princess from a neighboring village, she realized she would never be able to reason with her. The other princess insisted she was crazy and that no crops were missing. The princess knew she had to outsmart the other princess in order to save her village's crops. It was time the other princess got a taste of her own medicine. So one night, after all the villagers had fallen asleep, the princess sent her soldiers to the neighboring village. The soldiers quickly captured the village's crops and neatly stashed them away in the forest. The next morning the princess waited for word from the other princess.

By the time the sun had reached its highest point in the sky the other princess from the neighboring village had come. She asked the princess if she knew the whereabouts of her village's crops. The princess told her that if she promised to make sure no one from her kingdom would ever steal crops from the princess's land again, she would tell her where her crops were. It was a deal. After that, no one ever heard from the princess from the neighboring village or her ravaging villagers again.

It was a simple story, but it reminded me of me. Maybe that's why I thought I could stop this whole mess. The crazy part about it was that I had. Somehow, the end of the night was here, and I was in bed. Maybe not my bed but in bed nevertheless, and the drama was over. I learned about courage from that story. Now I knew just how much courage I had. I was proud of myself.

Chapter 14

I was strolling across the school, heading from the college office to my locker. This was my last day as a high school senior. Yes! It felt great, like the world was ahead of me. I had completed all the tests and reports and filled out my college applications. I had never imagined what it would be like to be done. I had a real sense of accomplishment. Being here for four years had shown how much I had grown up. I was about to graduate!

I had just taken my last final exam. All that was left for me to do was to clear out my locker. Since we were in the no-man's land of lockers, only two staircases led to that part of the building. This was the last day of my inconvenient trek to my locker. Thank goodness!

On my way, I passed Mr. Sui's office. How odd. I saw Detective Smart standing outside the office talking and laughing with Mr. Sui. How did they know each other? As I got closer to the fast friends, I could overhear Mr. Sui inviting Detective Smart and his wife over to his house for dinner.

"I can't believe this place hasn't changed," Detective Smart said.

"Neither have the personalities. I get the same kids each semester, just with different faces," Mr. Sui said.

"You think criminals are any better?" Detective Smart asked.

Mr. Sui chuckled. Get a life. I wonder if the secret society existed when they went here. That would've been about twenty years ago. Hmmm. Talk about a legacy. Mr. Sui didn't seem like he would join some nondescript secret society. He wasn't a follow-the-leader type. But Detective Smart acted like he thought he used to be cool.

I was walking by them when Detective Smart spotted me. I hadn't heard much from him after I took care of business regarding the stalking issue. What was his deal? He hadn't called me or my mother to tell us he'd be at the school today. My guess was he didn't have any suspects.

"We'll talk, Harrison," Detective Smart said to Mr. Sui.

Harrison Sui? I hadn't seen that one coming.

"Hi, Nia. How are you?" Detective Smart asked.

"Well," I said.

"We're here today on official business for your case. We interviewed a potential suspect by the name of Michelle Washington. Do you recall giving her name as a potential suspect?"

Why was he wasting my time with these useless questions?

"Yes, I do," I said.

"Well, according to her and her friend they were both getting their hair done at the salon that evening so she couldn't have done it."

Was I supposed to believe that? I was right there when she got that bob. "Did you find out if she got a receipt for this alleged haircut, or did she conveniently pay cash?"

"We're going to look into this further. But don't worry. I have a gut feeling this thing is over for the most part."

"Really?"

"Yes, ma'am. And I got a thorough scolding from your

mother. Seems you didn't make it straight home that night. But you got there. Not my job to babysit. Especially not a teenager like yourself who's got basements to raid," Detective Smart said.

"What?" I asked. Did he know more than he was letting on?

"Good luck in college," he said.

Yeah, he might've heard about the raid, but obviously he was light years behind on the news about the bedroom brawl and the stalking collage! At the mere thought of that stalking board, I felt like 100 spiders were crawling all over my back.

I wondered that if Detective Smart was a member of the secret popular society, would he not blame Michelle for it? Cindy had insisted on not pressing charges, so Michelle would only be charged for breaking and entering if she was found guilty. Either way, it was apparent she was never going to be prosecuted. That was a word I should've thrown at Detective Smart—"prosecute." Were they looking to prosecute anyone? He would've probably dodged that by asking me more questions he knew the answers to or reassuring me that this was over. The more I thought about it, the more I was sure this was a conspiracy. Who could I tell? Without my cell phone, I felt like I was just toiling around aimlessly in what seemed like a teenager's life.

When I got upstairs, I began to wonder why Cindy would opt to have a locker here next to me. It was sort of a test. I mean, if we were going to remain friends, then she might still be at the lockers. I didn't want a showdown in front of everyone—meaning the nerds, misfits, and well-dressed freshmen who were steadily taking over no-man's land lockers to claim it as their own area. I just wanted to talk.

So this was me, cleaning out my locker at a snail's pace. I

was playing it passive-aggressive, waiting for Cindy to drop by. Three trips to the trash can and a slow walk to the bathroom right next door to check my makeup, the weather outside, how I looked in my jeans, and, well, I was all done. Maybe when my cell privileges were back and my pride let up, I would call Cindy.

I left through the back entrance of the classroom. I felt compelled to turn around and take one last look.

"Nia!"

I turned around. To my surprise, Cindy was behind me. I jumped back. She looked as lost as I felt.

"Before you give me your spiel on how I betrayed you, listen. I know I should have admitted that I was part of the society. I had no right pretending and stuff. But I was trying everything I could to get it to stop. You have to believe me," she said.

"I do," I said.

"If I would've said something, you would've blamed me for all of those things that were happening. You hate everybody who's popular so much. I didn't know if we would even be friends anymore," Cindy said.

"I don't hate the popular. You make it sound like I'm discriminating," I said.

"No, I'm not. Part of the society rules is to keep it a secret. I was your friend, but I still had to follow the rules to the society I pledged. You have to know, I had no idea it would go that far. At first I was upset that you thought I was just your friend for that club. I would never do that. I was totally your friend. You're my best friend," Cindy said.

"Good, because I'm still your best friend," I said.

"That was easy. I was prepared to be screamed at. Poor

Jason." Cindy laughed.

"Jason?" I said, confused. I shook my head. Poor me. He was trouble for me. I never planned on having a sweet spot for him.

"He's perfect for you. I don't want to hear another word about it," Cindy said.

She sounded so mature. What had happened to her over the past week?

"And what up's with Peter? Are you two an item?" I laughed. Who the heck says "item" anymore? Spending the entire week at home with my mom was having a devastating effect on my vernacular.

Cindy cleared her throat and tugged uncomfortably at her sweater dress. "No! He decided to go to prom with a junior," she said.

"You're kidding me. We're graduating! What does he think he's trading up for a newer model?"

"I did like him. He was like ... I don't know. I can't even make an analogy. I thought he was different. My bad."

"What a loser."

"There were some problems. I didn't want to do it again until prom, to make it special, you know. And I don't know. It bothered him."

I'd never seen Cindy like this, self-reflective and maybe even a little insecure. She almost always got to dump the guy first. I felt a little bad for her. I had been there before. Peter was fool's gold. There were times when all the dating tricks and flirting in the world couldn't change how things were going to end up.

"I happen to know a hot guy that is dying to worship you."

"Really! Say it isn't so!" Cindy perked up.

"Are you going to start on your locker?" I laughed.

"I think the only thing I'm really going to take is my makeup and my lock," she said.

"Did you bring an overnight bag?"

"For what?"

"Your makeup," I said.

"You know, there are two things of mine you don't mess with: my man and my makeup. I have to be fly-i-i-i-i-i," she said.

She unleashed the beast inside her locker. Three Ziploc bags full of every type of cosmetic under the sun in all shapes, sizes, colors, and brands fell out. I bent down to help clean up the mess. A bronzer case fell right onto my head.

"That itty-bitty supermarket shopping bag will not do. But I know somebody who probably has everything we need in his locker," I said.

"Uh, you think Jason is your superhero. Ha! Ha! Nia and Jason sitting in a tree, k-i-s-s-i-n-g. First comes love, then come marriage... ," she said.

"Shut up! I was not talking about Jason. And who said anything about love?"

"I know love when I see it. It's everything I try to avoid," she said.

"You had me fooled. You were all ... 'I really liked him and he didn't want to wait,'" I said.

"Talk to the hand." Cindy put her hand in my face, which

would've been an appropriate response if it were 1990. Obviously, she'd seen one too many *In Living Color* reruns.

"I'm referring to Roger. Please just call the boy. Get him to help you lug this stuff home. I have to walk home with my boyfriend."

"Roger? … Maybe."

"Wait. You mean, you are going to call Roger?"

"Yeah." Cindy shrugged. This was truly the end of an era.

"You dig the makeover?" I asked.

Cindy busted out into a crazy sinister laugh. Had she and Roger already hooked up … or … "Are you seeing Roger?"

"No." She smiled.

"But you thought about it."

"No … okay, yeah," she said.

"Wow, just like that."

There was hope in life. Nothing was permanent—just look at Roger. Knowing that somehow made me feel like I would sleep better at night. You could become anything and change was always happening for the better.

"Plus, he thinks I'm smart," Cindy said. She voice-activated his number from her address book. Unbelievable. I hugged Cindy.

"I'm going to go. I, um … have a date. Stop by my house tomorrow during usual visiting hours."

"While your mom is at work?"

"You know it."

Chapter 15

"Michelle just came on too strong," a deep voice with a slight nervous crackle said from behind me. It almost caught me for a moment, like a sticky spider web. There was some sort of neurological reaction I had, in which he would speak and I used to flash a coy grin without even thinking.

I could even remember the first time he'd kissed me. I smiled. But my stint of brief reminiscing was quickly cleared away as he uttered, "Once she called you, I knew you figured we had hooked up."

I actually hadn't figured out immediately that Craig had hooked up with her. I'd hoped it was all some type of bad thing ... you know, the kind of thing that involved drinking or smoking or something that would cloud one's judgment. I could believe that he'd made a bad choice. I just couldn't believe he would break my heart. He'd once said to me, "I'm loving you." What did that mean? I should've figured out then that he had a few screws loose.

I didn't get the hint until Cindy had come to pick me up the next morning and showed me the overnight gossip texts. Then I knew what that meant. He didn't love me, he was just loving me—and whoever else came along, I suppose. I'd had a lot of doubt about his loyalty to me during our relationship. Craig continued ranting on and on. But I couldn't hear him. I couldn't see past all of the stupid things he had done to hurt me. So I just stood there, frozen and immobilized by shock.

Had he been waiting all month to say this? You know, people take common courtesies for granted. I didn't have to acknowledge his presence. I didn't have to listen to him. I felt like it was too bad for him. He should've tried the day after the phone call. Let's just call it what it was: the most embarrassing call ever.

"I couldn't find you for the next two weeks," he continued.

I looked him right in the eye. He had the nerve to act as if he had tried to redeem himself but I was underneath a rock or something. So he didn't get a proper opportunity. Please!

"I didn't move," I said. The resentment dripped from my lips which he couldn't stop staring at.

"I know it's over!" he shouted.

"You're getting way too serious about this," I said.

"School ... us. I don't—I don't know. I can't get you off my mind," he said.

It finally hit me. I would never get to be angry at him again. After graduation he would be a blip on the roadmap of my life. Good, because honestly he didn't even deserve that. This was the first time we'd spoken since he'd kissed me goodbye on my doorstep the same night I had been dumped.

"You're like my whole high school memory. The good thing I remember. I'll remember you sitting in the bleachers cheering us on," he said.

"That was one time!" I said. Enough of this melodrama, half of it didn't even make sense.

By now I could see exactly how ridiculous he was. What college was he going to anyway? I mean he didn't take any AP classes. So I guess he'd done me a favor. I'd gotten an upgraded model with new technology. It was like comparing one of those old cell phones that looked like a walkie-talkie to a new one that was razor-thin with Internet capabilities. He took a deep breath, and then he did the unthinkable.

"I know breaking up with you was the stupidest thing I did all year." Was he repenting? After all this!

"Don't pretend you're not shallow because you found a soul now that your reign is over and you realize in college you'll just be a number. One of tens of thousands of kids, many of whom will be more senior than you. You hooked up with Ms. Most Likely to Be in a Padded Room in Ten Years because she told you to. But that was all you!" I said.

"That was really stupid. I just said that," he said under his breath. He sighed. Then he wiped his face with his mammoth man hands, perfect for catching a football. He looked like a preacher caught with his hands in the cookie jar—namely, one of the deacon's wives. Church drama was much like high school drama.

"We would've never worked past high school anyway! I can't stand a guy that's whipped. I can only wonder if I meant all this to you when you were shacked up with Michelle."

"Forgive me!" Craig blurted out.

"You do dumb things all the time. People can't forgive you for every single dumb thing you've ever done," I said.

"I admitted it was stupid," he said.

"Is that the only part that was stupid? 'Cause this part, the part where you approach me six weeks later to talk about the break-up, ranks pretty high up there."

"Because you're smarter than me, does that make you

better than everyone?" he said.

"That doesn't even make sense. This is not about who's smarter. I'm loyal. People aren't disposable to me."

My cell phone buzzed with a new text message. Thank goodness. This was getting old. "That's probably my new boyfriend." I shrugged.

I walked away briskly. I wasn't sure what he wanted from me. A hug, approval ... maybe he wanted me to say it was okay to screw me over in the last quarter of the final game. Well, I wasn't going to do any of that. It took me long enough to get over this. Plus, he lucked out. I'm the one who shared a secret part of me. What I shared with him I could never get back. I did it because I thought we'd meant something. A girl shouldn't want that back anyway. Maybe that was what this was about, being at peace with what we'd shared. More like what I'd shared. He, on the other hand, had gladly doled himself out to more than a few other girls in our class, I'm sure.

I realized he had done me a favor by breaking up with me. I'd thought it all along, but I didn't feel it was actually true until right then. Before I left the popular corridor for the last time, I had to have one last look at my past and what was behind me now.

There, in that hallway, I was leaving the girl who had once believed that people were honest and true and meant you well. Instead, the new me knew that people, even the ones closest to you sometimes did things that hurt you, and you had to be careful whom you trusted. I also knew now that shallowness was a rampant disease. Even I had caught a touch of it when I thought I was popular. Since when does who you date, who your friends are, and what you look like mean everything? Generally speaking, that is. My makeup mantra still holds true to the grave: A girl can't leave the house without a little base, mascara, and eyeliner.

I didn't understand why Craig had done something that he would regret so dearly. Yet again, too bad. Everything wasn't for me to understand. Unfortunately, a guy like Craig would spend a greater portion of his youth reminiscing about his golden years. Face it, he had peaked at seventeen.

"I wish you the best in college!" I said softly. My scolding tone had subsided. I'd succumbed to belief in good karma. One too many public television specials, I guess. I couldn't just leave without forgiving him. It was negative energy to hold on to the past.

"Goodbye," I said.

"Bye," he said.

Chapter 16

Whenever I saw Jason it felt like time stopped. My smile, my laugh, they were all different around him. Even the way I ran my fingers through my hair was different because I knew he was watching. There was a side of my life that was a private show that only he had a ticket to. He had touched my heart in a way it had never been touched before. It wasn't any one thing in particular—it was everything he had never said that I knew he meant because of the look in his eyes, the way he always opened the door for me, and the way he wanted to protect me.

The sun was illuminating right onto his gorgeous face. He was sporting a slight outline of a beard extending from his sideburns, dark rinse jeans, and a fresh white tee that hugged his muscles. I felt different about him.

"Hi there," he said.

"Hey, babe." I kissed him.

We sat at the front fountain in front of the school.

"For summer, where are you going?" I asked.

"Where you go, I will follow. That, and I got a job at my dad's firm as an intern," he said. He held me in his arms.

Carolina came walking out of the school doors. She came up to us. "What up, Jason?" she said. I guess she considered herself Jason's friend.

"Hey," he said.

"Hi, Carolina," I said.

"Hi?" Carolina said.

"Where are you off to?" I asked.

"To meet Derek," she said.

"Word?" Jason said.

"Why?" she asked.

"Doesn't he have a girlfriend?" I asked.

"No," she said.

"Are you excited about graduation?" I asked her.

"No. I'm excited about prom," she said.

"Good. Well, I'll see you around." I walked over to her and gave her a hug. She was stunned.

"Okay," she said.

"Bye," I said.

"Bye," Jason said. She walked away slowly.

"What was that?" Jason asked.

"What?" I said.

"I thought you guys were arch enemies," he said.

"I know, but it turns out she wasn't my real enemy at all," I said. If I could forgive Craig, anything was possible. Though I must admit, I even surprised myself with this one.

We walked around the front lawn. It would be the last time we would.

"Are you going to remember me?" I asked.

"What do you mean?"

"Ten years from now, when you think back about high school, will you think of me?"

www.CameoTheNovel.com

"You? You're, like, from another planet. I'll definitely remember you."

"I was just thinking the same thing about you," I said.

His hands came at me with his fingers moving rapidly like the winds of a twister.

I screamed out. "Ah! No, no. Do not tickle me," I said.

His fingers tickled my body like a pianist tickles ivory keys. I burst out into laughter. My body convulsed defensively. He laughed, taking pleasure in torturing me with his touch. There was a permanent grin on my face from ear to ear. He picked me up in his arms and swung me around.

"Put me down, silly."

"You're crazy."

"No, you're crazy."

"Only since I met you."

I was close enough to him for our noses to touch. I tilted my head like I was going to kiss him, and then I whispered in his ear, "Check."

I started tickling him.

"Stop. Stop, Nia!"

"Beg for mercy."

"Nah." He laughed.

"Too bad." I continued to tickle him. He grabbed my hands. Suddenly I realized the tables had turned. He was going in for the kill.

"You better be ready for a rematch," Jason said.

I wiggled my arms every which way and struggled to get my hands free. Once I got them free, I ran across the street to the park. He chased me around the park for the rest of the afternoon. It was just me and my boyfriend.

If there wasn't such a thing as fool's gold, I guess one would never know the real thing. How could one tell what was fake? It felt like I had found something very close to the real thing. Every time he looked at me, I knew he felt the same way about me that he did the night he dropped me at my grandmother's house. And somehow his opinion was the only opinion that counted in the entire world. I never imagined it would be like this. And, yeah, I think he knew the look I had in my eyes. It was a look that said I could definitely have him for breakfast and maybe seconds for lunch. Good thing prom was in two days. Phew!

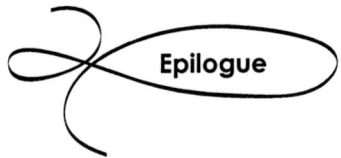

Epilogue

First things first: At prom, Jane had a secret she was itching to tell me. Dressed in a pink, backless metallic dress that came to just above her knees and with a fantastic high ponytail filled with soft curls, she looked like she had just stepped off the red carpet. But Jane was operating more like a publicist than a star. She was furiously tapping away at her Sidekick. She was definitely taking notes for the post-prom report.

"Hey, Nia! I love your black strapless with soft violet chiffon. I would've never thought of that," Jane said.

"It is fabulous, isn't it?" I said.

"So, I have a secret," Jane began.

It wasn't until that instant that I realized Jane was the type of girl who was going to keep tabs on everyone from high school for the next ten years, and come up with the reunion report.

She looked both ways in the hotel lobby. Then she inconspicuously pulled me behind a tall plant near the reception desk.

"I was going to take this to my grave." She paused.

Yeah, right. Not unless she was going to die in the next five minutes was this going to go to the grave with her. Jane could hold a secret about as well as a shopaholic could hold fifty bucks! I really hoped this had nothing to do with Jason because if she was going to take it to her grave I would've appreciated that more than knowing.

"I know you've been wondering," she whispered.

"Wondering what?"

"Who gave Roger the sexy biker boy makeover?"

"Yeah, kind of."

"Okay, he let me cheat off him on a bio quiz. Those damn quizzes count for like 40 percent of your grade and, well, I was tied up with Derek the night before," she said.

"Jason's friend, Derek? Doesn't he date Carolina?"

"No. He's with me now," Jane said sternly.

"I see," I said. Who was I to question her?

"Back to Roger. He told me he really, really liked Cindy, and he wanted me to help him get her. And she told me her ideal guy was a hot, clean-cut-by-day, bad-boy-by-night-looking guy with a motorcycle. I didn't study for the last three quizzes, if you know what I mean."

I arched my eyebrows so high they practically reached my hairline.

"Phat, right?" she asked.

"Hmmm," I said. What they say is true ... nothing is ever as it seems.

As for Michelle, she wasn't voted prom queen—something about a write-in vote who won by a landslide. Craig went with her to prom, though they didn't leave together. She left with Lucy. And Gary, I overheard him telling Roger how he met his prom date, Vala. How crazy is that?

I was never blacklisted from the yearbook. It's a funny thing, yearbook. Roger decided it was time MIA stood its ground and put up a fight. As co-president, he put to rest the urban myth that if one crossed the popular secret society they would be ousted from the yearbook and would probably not get a job in this town after college graduation. I found out about the last part a couple of days after we had given Michelle her makeover.

Someone had sent Gary a text about it, and he had forwarded to me. We just laughed about it. Seriously, there was life outside of this town. The smart, the un-inducted, and the inappropriately labeled "nerds" were no longer at the mercy of the popular secret society because a new story had been written at this school. This urban legend starred a girl who was neither popular nor a nerd but a superbly dressed, non-narcissist hybrid who ended up with the guy, the popular best friend, and a full page as the prom queen in the yearbook! If ever there was a moment for a high five, now would be it!

Forever, Nia

Order Undercover Starlet, Starlet Journal Today!
ISBN: 978-0-9787302-0-8

The *Undercover Starlet, Starlet Journal* is a colorful, inspirational diary for young women to write out their thoughts.

The *Starlet Journal* features an inspirational notes section with tips on how to feel good and take care of yourself everyday written by **Tanille**, author of the novel *Cameo*.

Dr. Latoya Edwards contributes a health article on nutrition and eating choices to remind young women to make better choices when nourishing their bodies. The *Starlet Journal* is a complete diary to help young women care for their minds, bodies, and souls.

Title: Undercover Starlet, Starlet Journal
ISBN: 978-0-9787302-0-8
Publisher: Fire Flies Entertainment LLC

Retail Price: $19.95

Contributors: Tanille Edwards & Latoya Edwards M.D.
Order at Barnes & Noble Stores and online at www.Amazon.com

www.CameoTheNovel.com

Children's Books by Tanille

Jordan & Justine's Weekend Adventures™: Go Go Green takes children on an exciting, high-flying adventure as they learn to go green. Jordan and Justine are part of a Go Go Green campaign in their community, and they teach young readers about the environment, how to take steps to save energy, how to participate in their community, and why it is important to care about the earth! The multicultural cast of characters in this book explores how Native American culture uses the environment for resources and how modern living affects the environment. Children will also learn new words in Spanish.

ISBN: 978-0-97873002-6-0

Jordan & Justine's Weekend Adventures™: Wildlife Parts 1 & 2
Available at your local bookstore and online at retailers everywhere. Children will love following Jordan and Justine on a wild adventure to a wildlife reserve where they use their imaginations and magic to learn about endangered animals.

ISBN: 978-0-9787302-4-6

Jordan & Justine's Weekend Adventures™: Plants Parts 1 & 2
Available at bookstores and online everywhere. Children learn about planting, healthy eating, and much more!

ISBN: 978-0-9787302-4-6

And now available in Spanish!

**Jordan & Justine's Weekend Adventures™:
Plantas Partes 1 & 2**

ISBN: 978-0-9787302-5-3

Available at bookstores and online everywhere.
www. JordanGoGreen.com

www.UndercoverStarlet.com

CPSIA information can be obtained at www.ICGtesting.com
Printed in the USA
BVOW08s2137080913

330515BV00001B/1/P